MW01601113

behind
the
stick

Copyright

If you are reading this book and did not purchase it or win it from an author sponsored giveaway, this book has been pirated. Please delete it from your device, and support the author by purchasing a legal copy from one of its many distributors.

No part of this book may be used or reproduced in any form or by any means electronic or mechanical, including photocopying, recording, or by any information storage and retrieval systems, without prior written permission of the author except where permitted by law.

Behind the Stick

Published by Sandra Marie

https://sandramarieauthor.wixsite.com/sweetsandra/

Cover Design: Makeready Designs

Editing: CookieLynn Publishing Services

Formatting: CookieLynn Publishing Services

The characters and events portrayed in this book are fictitious. Any similarity to real persons, living or dead is coincidental and not intended by the author.

Copyright © 2019 Sandra Marie

All rights reserved.

behind
the
stick

romance for all seasons #6

SANDRA MARIE

one

Lauren kicked off her ballet flats after a long day of working in the children's section of the local library, slipped on her black framed reading glasses, and plopped on her bed. Reaching under her pillow, she pulled out her latest read. It was a historical romance where the heroine ran away from home to avoid an unwanted marriage only to be swept up into a love affair with a pirate. The story was exhilarating and more romantic than anything Lauren had ever experienced by far.

It was why her relationship with Dylan didn't last. He simply failed in comparison to the heroes in her books. She knew she shouldn't hold men to such ridiculous standards, but why the hell not? He complained she always had her nose between the pages of a book, yet he never did anything interesting enough to make her put the book down. Besides, he was one to talk. He had his eyes glued to his cell phone, entirely obsessed with scrolling through social media or playing some stupid casino game. At least Lauren got to experience adventure every time she turned her attention to her book.

Though, the breakup still stung. It was just another failure on her list. Another reminder that the great love affair she always dreamed about would never happen.

Dylan was a good guy in the beginning, and she wanted

to love him, but it never happened. They weren't compatible, or it was possible Dylan was right and their failed relationship was all because she cared more about spending time with a book than having a conversation with him which he reminded her of multiple times while he ended things.

If only their conversation was interesting and engaging, instead of him complaining about life, then maybe she would have put the book down.

She was beginning to think that whole thing about butterflies in the stomach, heat coursing through her body, and an overwhelming desire to be close to someone was nothing more than pure fiction.

"Abigail, I will just have to live vicariously through you," she said to the cover before flipping to the page that held her bookmark.

She snuggled under her fleece blanket and rested against her pillows. At the end of the day, this was the only place Lauren wanted to be. She placed the bookmark on her nightstand and dove into the story. A few minutes later when things were starting to really pick up, there was a subtle knock on her bedroom door.

Just as Abigail fell into the arms of her pirate, Lauren looked up from the book and spotted Ginny, her old roommate and closest friend, awkwardly waving from the doorway. She had moved out only a few weeks ago to live with her boyfriend across the street. Lauren had told her to keep the key since it would always be her home—at least as long as Lauren continued to rent a room.

"Hey, Gin," Lauren said. She grabbed her bookmark

and placed it between the pages before putting the book down and sitting up. "What's going on?"

Ginny rested her hand against her thigh, dog hair sticking to her black tights. "Lily May invited us to meet up at the Hole in the Wall and you should come."

Lauren smiled at the ease in Ginny's speech. For so long, Ginny stuttered, not having the confidence to speak. Once they became close, it wasn't as noticeable, but there were still times when she'd get stuck on a word. Now she looked at Lauren as she spoke, not darting her eyes to the floor. Confidence looked good on her, or maybe it was just the high of being head over heels in love. But ever since Ginny opened her heart to the boy next door, she was happier, almost lighter. It couldn't have happened to a better person even if Lauren was a bit envious.

"It'll be fun," Ginny added. "Everyone is going to be there, Frankie and Alex, Rae and Tommy, Cassidy and Jon."

As the only single friend in the group, it sounded about as fun as a root canal. They would try to include Lauren into the conversations, but the couples would have their inside jokes that would have them lovingly smiling at each other as if no one else existed. It's not that it would be done on purpose either, it was what happened when you were in love with someone. She'd bet money they didn't even notice when they were doing it. Besides, she didn't have any homework, so she had even more time than usual to spend reading for pleasure.

Lately, by the time she'd get done with the work for the master's program she was taking so she could become a librarian, she was only able to get in a few chapters before falling asleep every night.

"I'm going to stay in and read." Abigail and her sexy pirate were the only company Lauren needed tonight.

"I think going out would be good for you." Ginny tucked a newly dyed green streaked strand behind her ear. Though it was only a single strand of color, it was Ginny's mark of rebellion. Sometimes the color coincided with the next holiday. Green was perfect since Saint Patrick's Day was just around the corner. Her finger lingered at the bottom of the strand, tugging at the ends. "You could use a little fun after…" Ginny's sentence died off.

Lauren didn't need her to finish. She could use a little fun after Dylan dumped her, told her she was boring, and she would never be happy with her fiction-based standards.

I'm sorry, but I want someone a little less… well boring. Dylan's words echoed in her mind, and she bit back the involuntary wince as they dug at her like a sharp knife to the back.

She smiled at Ginny, grateful for a friend like her, but tonight she wanted to wallow in self-pity for a little while longer while reading about someone else falling in love and if that made her boring, she didn't care.

"I appreciate the invite, but I'm fine. Really. You go and have a great time. You can even leave Cocoa here with me." Lauren knew Ginny hated leaving her beloved pup alone, even if it did have two hyper companions in the aptly named Batman and Robin, but really, Lauren wouldn't mind a little fuzzy company to curl up with. Besides, Cocoa never thought she was boring.

The sound of the front door opening and closing echoed through the house. Steven, Ginny's boyfriend, breezed in and came to a stop next to Ginny, tossing his arm around her shoulders.

"We going?" he asked. "I corralled all the dogs in the kitchen and fed them, then slipped out the back. Batman spotted me and almost made a break for it, but luckily he was more interested in his kibble."

"Lauren doesn't want to go." Ginny shrugged, and Steven's arm fell from her shoulder. He cocked a dark eyebrow and stared Lauren down. Ginny would have been easy to get rid of, but Steven was a completely different story. Proving his character, he stepped toward the bed and plucked the book right out of Lauren's hand.

"Hey, give that back." She attempted to grab it, but he held it above his head and even if she were to try and get it back, she'd never reach it. She flumped onto the bed, and he tucked the book inside his jacket.

He smirked. "I will give it to you when we get home."

"That's a dirty play," she said.

"Desperate times call for desperate measures."

"It is not desperate times."

His eyes softened, concern pulling at the corners. "Since Dylan broke up with you, you go to work and come home. You're going to be permanently imprinted in that mattress soon."

"Am not." She appreciated his concern, she did, but it wasn't like she went out much when she was with Dylan anyway. Maybe she did leave the house a little more often, but sheesh, she just got dumped. Couldn't she have a week of moping? "I go to book club still."

"The book club held right there in your living room." He pointed behind him. "Another room in the house does not count."

She stubbornly crossed her arms over her chest. "Well, it should."

"Come for one drink, and if after one drink, you're not feeling it, I'll get you an Uber, and you can come back here and read until your heart's content."

"I'd rather just do that now."

"You're killing me!" Steven threw his hands up in an overly dramatic gesture.

"Let's just leave her be," Ginny said.

Steven let out a sigh. "Fine."

"See you later." With a sympathetic wave, Ginny followed Steven out the door.

Grateful Steven didn't sit there until she agreed, she repositioned herself and reached for her book. Only problem was it wasn't there.

"Steven!"

A loud laugh belted out from across the house. "You have five minutes to get dressed."

If she wanted to find out if Abigail would ever tell her sexy pirate the truth about where she came from, Lauren had no choice. She was going out whether she wanted to or not.

Lauren's idea of getting dressed was slipping back into her ballet flats. She didn't even bother to look in a mirror to see if her eye makeup had lasted through the day or if her hair needed a good brush. If she was a little less self-conscious, she would have changed into a pair of cozy pajamas and slippers. Unfortunately, the no mirror thing was the extent of her going out when she didn't want to protest.

Her dress had wrinkles in it from curling up in bed, and her black tights had shifted awkwardly giving her a permanent wedgie. She did a bit of weebling to get those suckers back in alignment before walking out the front door and slipping into the backseat of Steven's car.

Ginny handed her a lint roller. "You'll need this when you get out. We took the dogs to the dog park, and someone forgot to vacuum the backseat."

"I have no idea what you're talking about," Steven said as he pulled out onto the street. Ginny smiled adorably at him.

Ginny and Steven fell into a conversation about work for the ASPCA and Lauren, not able to add anything to the conversation, pulled out her cell to scroll through her Kindle app.

She had about four books started that she jumped between whenever she had time to kill. She decided on a non-fiction book about building confidence. Not that she felt she really needed to build her confidence, but after the breakup, she thought it wouldn't hurt. When she was ready, she would have to put herself out there again, and since she veered on the side of socially awkward, any little bit of advice was helpful.

Fifteen minutes later, they drove by the bar and found a

spot on the street. Steven parallel parked with ease, and Lauren took the time to thoroughly go over her black tights with the lint roller before passing it to Ginny.

The Hole in the Wall was exactly that—a bar front with no bells and whistles, just a sign above the door with its name and a free-standing sign on the sidewalk that listed the happy hour specials. Lauren had heard of the place now owned by Gavin Mills, the brother of Seattle's richest man, Ashton Mills, who was Lily May's boyfriend, but she had never met Gavin. Though if he was Ashton Mills twin, then he was definitely good looking. Lauren couldn't imagine the world being graced with two men with that bone structure.

She followed Steven and Ginny through the door, the place was small, a few tables scattered about and black leather stools lined the bar. There was a random roped off corner under construction with a half taken down wall full of wires. The rest of the décor looked like it hadn't been updated since the Space Needle was erected.

Lauren scanned the rest of the place, taking in the old wood planks beneath her feet as they made their way away from the door and closer to the bar. She spotted the man behind the bar just as he spotted her. His eyes turned to her, bright green and beautiful, and he smiled. It was warm, friendly, and welcoming, and though she imagined he greeted all the guests with that exact same tilt of the lips, for some reason an excited jilt rushed through her. Her cheeks heated, and her head darted down.

There was no question the gorgeous man was Gavin Mills and the world had definitely been graced twice when he and his brother were born.

He looked different than Ashton though, not nearly as proper or rigid. He had an ease with the way he moved around the bar like it was almost a part of him. His face was clean shaven unlike Ashton who liked to keep a permanent five o'clock shadow.

"Hello there," he said and Lauren smiled as if she suddenly forgot how to speak. She cleared her throat ready to force the words out when Steven reached across the bar and shook Gavin's hand.

"Hey man, how's it going?" Steven asked and after a beat Gavin took his eyes from her and answered Steven.

Lily May hurried over to them from where Rae and Tommy were at a table, in her bright pink dress pants with a white sheer shirt tucked in. Not many people could pull off such a bright color, but when someone looked like she walked right out of a Barbie box, it was as if clothes like that were made for her.

"You made it!"

"We did." Ginny gave Lily May a hug before Lily May smacked a kiss on Steven's cheek.

"Lauren!" Lily May exclaimed with a little too much exuberance, her voice echoing through the entire place. The other people in the bar looked in their direction briefly before going back to their conversations. Lily May didn't even notice as she drew Lauren in for a hug. She pulled back, resting her hands on Lauren's arms. "I can't believe you came!"

Lauren shot a glance in Steven's direction, then down

to the inside pocket of his coat where he held her book hostage. "I didn't really have a choice," she said. "But now that I'm here, I'm happy I came." She glanced over at the bar where Gavin was handing over a pint glass. He caught her eye and gave her a wink. Lauren quickly snapped her attention away, but it wasn't quick enough. Lily May's eyebrow shot up, a spark ignited in her big blue eyes.

"Let me introduce you to Gavin." Lily May grabbed her hand and pulled her to the bar. For a petite thing she sure had an iron grip. Defenseless, Lauren followed, plastering on a smile.

"Gavin!" Lily May called and waved.

He excused himself from the conversation he was having and strolled over to where they stood at the bar. "I wanted you to meet my friend Lauren."

Lauren gave an awkward wave.

"Nice to meet you," he said, holding his hand out.

She swallowed, then reached out to accept. His hand dwarfed hers as he gave it a strong shake. Their eyes met, and now that she was close, she could see the different shades of green that made up the beautiful color.

"Isn't she just as cute as a peach?" Lily May said, and Lauren froze, heat creeping up her neck.

Gavin smiled. "Cuter," he said, and to keep herself from looking like a pathetic school girl with a crush, she yanked her hand away and forced herself to get a grip.

"It's nice to meet you," she said finally remembering how to form words, then glanced around the bar and watched as Lily May sneakily left them alone. "Great place you have here." Though it was a lie considering the eyesore that was the construction, she could see the potential.

Pride shown in the deep green of his eyes. "Thanks. It needs a little TLC, but I'm working on it."

The bell above the door sounded, and the infamous Ashton Mills stepped inside. He looked around the bar, a glint in his eyes like he was desperate to find someone, but then his gaze lingered on the construction. His eyebrows furrowed and he changed direction, heading straight to the bar.

"This place looks like a shithole," Ashton said to Gavin before he even sat down on a stool. "What the hell happened?"

Gavin's friendly disposition distorted, and Lauren thought it best to remove herself from the glaring eyes and tight jawlines.

She excused herself and found a stool at the end of the bar. Steven's coat hung on a hook, and she reached inside, grabbing her book.

It was time to forget about her own loveless life and catch up with Abigail. She opened the book and glanced toward Gavin again. His shoulders were tense and she imagined what it would be like to massage the tension away. She quickly swatted that thought away. She was fresh off a breakup and the last thing she needed was to start fantasizing about another guy, who with that charming wink he'd given her, had heartbreaker written all over him.

 # two

Gavin suppressed the desire to throw his rag at his brother's smug face and took a deep breath instead. "It's called construction," he said through clenched teeth. It was so typical of Ashton to shoot him down right as a pretty girl was lifting him up. Ashton was so good at it he didn't even know when he was doing it.

"I told you to call *my* contractor. This would have been done weeks ago."

If he called Ashton's contractor, then Ashton would know every single thing that was wrong with the place ever since Gavin decided to start messing with things. If Gavin would have just left things the way they were, he could've continued to be blissfully unaware of how much of a dump this bar was beneath the walls and floorboards.

He had visions of what this bar could be and those ideas slipped away the minute the random wall in the far side of the bar revealed its actual purpose and the costly nightmare that hid beneath.

In order to finish the construction, it would cost more money that Gavin didn't have, and he'd already be paying Ashton back for the rest of his life with the loan he took from him to buy this place; the last thing he wanted to do was add to the debt.

It had taken everything he had to walk into Ashton's million-dollar office overlooking Seattle and ask for money. He swore to himself when he stepped out of the office that he would never ask his brother for another penny.

Unfortunately, he was already nose deep where Ashton was concerned. He refused to tell his brother that he couldn't afford to pay the contractors. He would never hear the end of it. Ashton would lecture him on financial bullshit that would make him feel like an idiot for jumping in blindly. Nope, no way in hell he was about to throw himself in front of that bus.

Luckily, Lily May, tapped Ashton on the shoulder, and he focused on her.

"Hello to you too," she said, her hand landing on her hip, annoyance radiating off of her in amusing waves.

"Sorry, baby," he said, drawing her in for a quick kiss.

She patted his chest. "Now that's more like it."

Ashton stared at her with nothing but adoration and Lily May knew it.

"Look at you grinning like a possum eating a sweet potato," she said, her own lips curving upward.

"I have a lot to grin about." Ashton grabbed her around the waist and Lily May let out a high-pitched squeak.

"Must you do that? You're going to scare my customers away," Gavin joked while he got down a bottle he kept aside for Ashton. He'd never seen his brother's intimidating nature fade so quickly. It usually took a few glasses of top shelf scotch to achieve any ease to his uptight posture and stoic expression.

"What customers?" Ashton asked, and Gavin bit his tongue…hard.

Lily May's blonde hair spun around her as she twirled to face Gavin. Her eyebrow lifted. "Now don't go and get your feathers ruffled on me." She gave him a quick smile, and he smiled back a thank you for defusing the situation.

Gavin held his hands up. "No feathers here to ruffle." He poured the amber liquid in a glass and pushed it toward Ashton. Maybe a few sips of scotch would lighten his ass up a little more and he'd leave Gavin the hell alone. The last thing Gavin wanted to deal with tonight was Ashton's inability to let things go. Lily May had invited all of their friends here and Gavin was looking forward to catching up with everyone, especially getting more acquainted with Lauren, without Ashton's disappointed glare constantly wandering in his direction. Lily May gave a sassy tilt of her head, then clapped her hands together, looking from Ashton then to Gavin. "So what'd I miss here?"

"Nothing," he and Ashton said at the same time.

"That tells me that's a lie." Lily May pointed her finger at them.

"Did you just Maury Povich us?" Gavin asked.

Lily May laughed. "Maybe. Neither of you are trying to figure out who the baby daddy is of the pregnant woman you're both seeing, I still thought it was fitting…. but if nothing is going on." She leaned in closer to the bar and gave a motion with her head to the far corner opposite the construction. "Why don't we talk about Lauren?"

Gavin refrained from rolling his eyes. Lily May was

14

determined to set him up on dates ever since she found out that he signed up for an online dating site. He did it out of desperation. With Ashton's annual charity gala coming up, and with Ashton happily attached to Lily May, he couldn't show up to the party without a date. If he did, his dads would never stop questioning him about when he was planning on settling down. The two men were getting impossible in their old age. Just because they were blissfully happy together since their late twenties, they expected everyone else to be.

For the most part, they left Ashton alone since he was building his legacy, and Gavin would get the brunt of the concerned parent brigade, using their favorite go to line, *we just want you to be happy.*

Now that Ashton had it all, the empire that expanded more and more every day and the beautiful girlfriend who was nicer than any human Gavin had ever known, Ashton was once again making Gavin look bad.

If he could show up to the gala with a date on his arm then he'd be free of the questions. Online dating proved to be a bust though. When he finally had a match worth a dime, it turned out she was madly in love with her best friend. Rae and Tommy belonged together though, and, as if she knew he was thinking about her, Rae caught his eye from across the way where she stood with Steven and Ginny and gave him a wave. He nodded in acknowledgment, getting her and Tommy's drinks together, virgin rum and Cokes, while Lily May practically burned a hole in the side of his head.

"Gavin Mills, you cannot ignore me."

"Want to make a bet," he said, and Ashton cracked a smile.

"I really think you and Lauren would be perfect for each other."

"That's what you said about Darla from your spin class who told me every single nutritional fact of everything I put in my mouth. Then there was Becca you met at the dog park, which I still don't understand why you were at a dog park when you don't even have a dog."

"I do, in North Carolina."

"Yes," Gavin said. "But that still doesn't explain why you would be in a dog park here."

"Fine, I like to pet them. Is there anything wrong with that?"

Gavin laughed before looking at his brother. "Can you get the girl a dog?"

"I don't need him to get me anything," Lily May declared, her head tilting upward. "Besides, there's a no pet rule in my building."

"Yes, but he owns the building," Gavin said, hitching his thumb in Ashton's direction. "I'm sure he'd make an exception."

She waved her hand in front of her. "Stop trying to get me off track with your puppy distractions. Becca was a very nice girl."

"She was, but there wasn't one thing on her face that was real. And, hey, if you like that sort of thing by all means go for it, but I prefer a natural beauty."

"Okay, so she wore a lot of makeup and is a little heavy

on the contouring."

"A lot? I couldn't tell if I was talking to a person or a painting."

"Fine, so she wasn't your type. What about Tara from my bank? What was wrong with her?"

"Other than the fact that she asked about your boyfriend every other sentence."

A storm brewed in Lily May's blue eyes, turning them dark. "What!?"

"Yeah, it seems she was more obsessed with the fact that I was Ashton Mills brother than anything else."

"Well, you are lucky for that," Ashton said, and Gavin finally tossed the rag at his head.

Ashton caught it before it could slap him in the face and shook his head as he placed it on the bar. "Real mature."

Gavin shrugged. He spotted an empty glass in front of one of his regulars. "While I would love to stand here and chat some more, I have customers I have to help." Gavin swiped the rag up and flopped it over his shoulder. "And you invited all your friends here," he said to Lily May. "Go have fun, tell Rae I have her drinks, and don't worry about my dating life."

"But—"

"Let him be," Ashton said, taking her in his arms and guiding her toward the group of their friends.

She peeked around Ashton. "This isn't over," she called out, and Gavin laughed. He didn't need her to tell him. Lily May was anything if not determined and for whatever reason she was fixated on setting him up.

Gavin filled Devin's glass and bullshitted with him about a few of the local breweries that had popped up in the area. It was bad enough Gavin was competing with the new sports bar around the corner, but now he was also competing with breweries. While he had no hope of winning against a sports bar stacked with twenty-two TVs and a beer selection that would rival a distributor, he wanted to find a way for him and the breweries to work together.

There was one thing Gavin loved, and that was beer, and he wanted his bar to show that. Granted he would still carry all the other staples, like his brother's top shelf scotch, wine, and mixed drinks, but he also wanted to carry craft beers that were growing mass appeal. He had ideas. Hundreds of ideas that he wanted to implement like having the breweries do a tap takeover, offering a discount if the brewery sent someone over to him, hosting a cask festival, and even having live music and trivia nights. The problem was, with all this never-ending construction, potential customers took one look at the place and walked out.

He never should have tried to knock down that wall in the corner. Now he knew it contained half the wiring in the place, but that didn't help him now. He thought just reconstructing another wall would fix the problem, but once the contractor saw the shoddy wires, he advised to update the wiring and adding a bigger expense that Gavin couldn't afford, but also something he couldn't ignore either. The last thing he needed was one of those wires to cause a fire.

It kept him up at night, and since he lived in the apartment upstairs, he would come down to the bar and check everything a few times a night. He'd barely been sleeping because of it.

He looked at his brother, who was finally lightening up, then over at the under-construction portion of his bar. Maybe he should just ask Ashton for the money and be done with it. He already owed him a fortune, so what was a few thousand more at this point?

Still there was something inside him, pride most likely, that kept him from marching over there and asking Ashton to talk. Instead he pushed all thoughts out of his head and focused his attention on Devin until he got up to use the bathroom.

Gavin could easily go over to the group that he now called his friends, but he wasn't feeling very social at the moment. Everyone over there was in a happy relationship, thriving at life, and he was forever stuck in the habitual phase of never getting it right.

He went to lean against the bar when he noticed Lauren still hiding in the corner, her nose burrowed deep in a book, long brown hair hanging over the side of her face.

"Reading anything good?" he asked as he approached.

"It's not bad," she said, not even bothering to glance up at him.

"That good, huh?"

She held her finger up, and he stifled a laugh as her eyes roamed the page before gently closing the book and placing it down on her lap. She pushed a pair of black plastic frame glasses up her nose, and he couldn't bite back the smile at the adorable bookworm in front of him.

"I didn't mean to keep you from the good parts," he said. "I know how annoying that can be."

Her head tilted. "You read?"

He reached behind the bar, pulling out a worn copy of his favorite book. "As often as I can."

Amusement flashed across her pretty features. "Did you just pull a book out from under the bar?"

"Why, did you find it wildly attractive? I can do it again." Gavin put the book back then grabbed it, holding it up with renewed vigor.

Her forehead creased. "Do you really think the book is what makes you attractive?"

"So what you're saying is that you think I'm hot."

"What I'm saying is my boyfriend and I just broke up, and I am not ready for whatever it is you're attempting." She wiggled her finger between them before placing her hand on her lap with the book.

"Have you had your nose in that book so long you've forgotten how to communicate with fellow humans?"

Her eyebrows drew together, creating a cute look of confusion. "What is that even supposed to mean?"

"That maybe I wasn't flirting. Maybe I was just being friendly because you're over here by yourself, and as a good bartender, it is my job to make sure you're okay."

A disappointed glint flashed in her eyes. "So you weren't flirting with me?"

"No, I totally was."

She laughed, and the sound was a mix between sunshine and hot chocolate, both warm and welcoming after a cloudy day. "I appreciate your honesty," she said.

"Don't be fooled by my forwardness; it's just that I've never really been a good liar. I don't have that stoic face like my brother."

"You say that like it's a bad thing," she said. "But it's not."

"Why are you over here all by yourself?" he asked, looking toward the group of their mutual friends.

She lifted one shoulder and let it fall, her brown hair lifting and falling with the movement. "Like I said I just went through a breakup and being around all those happy couples is…"

"Depressing?" he asked.

The sad lines around her mouth vanished as she glanced up and met his gaze. "Exactly."

He leaned against the bar, ignoring the mess he couldn't fix and the brother he loved but would never beat, and sunk into the conversation with the adorable bookworm.

"I might not be going through a breakup, but I get it. Being the only single guy in a group makes me feel like a total fish out of water."

"Yes! I mean not that I'm a guy but it's the same thing for girls too. When your friends are in relationships things change and I know they don't mean to have their inside jokes that leave the rest of us feeling left out."

"Or to talk about how happy they are and all the new exciting things they have planned."

"Exactly. It comes with the territory, but coming off another failed relationship, I don't want to be reminded about how I can't seem to find that happily ever after no matter how hard I've tried."

"That's the thing," he said. "When it comes to the happily ever after stuff, you shouldn't have to try so hard. It should just happen."

"When you least expect it, right? At least that's what everyone says."

His eyes met hers. "I think they may be on to something."

***

Lauren had no idea how much time had passed since she and Gavin started talking, but for the first time in her life, she didn't care. She wasn't thinking about going home, crawling into bed, and losing herself in a book. She was enjoying losing herself in this conversation.

Gavin was nothing like Dylan, thank god. He looked at her when he spoke, genuinely listened to what she had to say, and never once picked up his phone while she was talking to him. It was a refreshing change of pace, and Lauren enjoyed not only the attention, but the company.

Gavin pointed at her, smile spreading wide across his face. "Most embarrassing memory, shoot."

"I'm not telling you that," she said as she sipped the blueberry wheat beer Gavin suggested when she told him she liked herbal teas. The beer tasted nothing like her favorite tea by any means, but it wasn't bad either.

"Oh, come on, don't go getting shy on me now," he said, and her chin dipped down.

For the most part, Lauren kept to herself; she wasn't exactly shy, but she wasn't outgoing either, at least not until she had a chance to warm up to someone. With Gavin though, the ease was almost instant, and while she would never tell anyone this horribly embarrassing story, she wanted to tell him.

"Excuse me, Gavin" A guy at the end of the bar held up his hand.

"I'll be right back," Gavin said.

Lauren went to reach for her book, but instead focused her attention on Gavin. She watched as he took the guys empty glass and without asking for a reminder of what he was drinking, began to refill it. He engaged in small conversation asking the guy about his kid's karate match.

It was obvious Gavin loved being a bartender and he was good at it. He seemed to know his customers and genuinely care about them and their lives.

When he handed over the glass, a woman came up to bar and flashed him a big smile. "You're hot," she said and Gavin bashfully smiled.

"Thanks, can I get you something else? A water maybe?"

She waved her hand at him, eyes pinched closed as she swayed. "How about your number."

"Silvia, we're leaving," a redhead said, tapping her friend on the shoulder.

"Raincheck on the water," Silvia said and gave Gavin a sloppy wink before stumbling away. Silvia and her friends disappeared into the night and Gavin came back to Lauren.

"Sorry about that," he said.

"No worries, you're working. I shouldn't be holding you up like this anyway especially when you have customers or should I say a fan club."

He laughed, loud and boisterous, the sound filling her with joy. "No fan club and don't think you're going to get out of telling me your most embarrassing memory."

An uncontrollable grin pulled at her mouth. "I was hoping you'd forget."

"Not in a million years." He clapped his hands together. "Now what it is? The suspense is killing me here."

She took a deep breath and let it out slowly. "I wet my pants at a sleepover when I was ten. I was scared to get up in the middle of the night to go to the bathroom and didn't want to wake anyone up."

Amusement danced across his face. "So you just peed your pants?"

"I know it seems ridiculous now, but that hallway was creepy. Seriously, it gave off *The Shinning* vibes. I expected to walk out of that room and see the twins standing at the end of the hallway asking me to play with them."

Gavin smirked. "What's wrong with twins?"

"Nothing is wrong with twins as long as you can blink without their dead bodies being slain across a hallway and their blood dripping down the walls."

"I gather you're not a fan of horror movies then?"

"Not really. The world is terrifying enough. When I watch a TV show or read a book, I want to escape the hardships and sadness."

24

"The world isn't all that scary though. You just have to look in the right places."

"That's easier for some people," she said, trying to hide the years of disappointment in her voice. Being abandoned by her own parents when she was only a child made it hard for her to escape the sadness. She hated that after all these years, her parents still had an effect on her, but when they made the choice not to want her, they had permanently broken a piece of her heart.

His eyes narrowed, and she felt like he was shining a spotlight above her head. "Not for you though?" he asked.

"I see what you're doing."

"What?" His head snapped back in confusion. "What am I doing?"

"Pulling that bartender mumbo jumbo on me. Asking me questions to get me to open up and give you more information without actually asking me."

He held one hand over his heart and the other up in front of him. "I wasn't doing it on purpose I swear."

"It's all right." He was a bartender and she was sure that curious nature to figure out someone's issues was in his blood. He probably dealt with more people's problems a day than a therapist. "Anybody else I wouldn't have acknowledged it and would have made a random subject change."

"So why haven't you?"

She shrugged. "I guess… I like talking to you."

A smile titled his lips. "I like talking to you, too."

Heat exploded in her cheeks, but she ignored the

sudden rush of shy joy. "It's your job to talk to people."

"Doesn't mean I enjoy everyone I speak to. Besides, most people don't care about me. They just need a sounding board to figure out their own problems. Usually, I just give them a few words of guidance, and they find their own way. Once they do, they never stick around to ask about me. They're gone before I can even say 'here's your change.'"

"But you love it anyway?"

"I do." It was obvious in the way he would stand back and look around the bar and smile. How he talked to everyone even the girl who tried to hide in the corner with a book. There was a tangible joy that flowed off of him when he stood behind that bar.

"Lauren, we have to get going," Ginny said, and Lauren's heart sunk a little. She went from not wanting to leave her bed to not wanting to return to it. Ginny waved to Gavin. "Bye, Gavin. It was good seeing you again."

"You too, Ginny. Take care."

"I'll just be over here," Ginny said, pointing to where Steven was saying goodbye to everyone. Cassidy and Jon were there. Lauren didn't even realize they had shown up and now she felt a little guilty for not acknowledging her friends. She hoped they'd understand and not hold it against her, though that definitely wasn't their style.

Lauren grabbed her purse and took out her wallet. Gavin held up his hand and waved her away. "On the house."

"No, I don't expect you to pay for my drink."

"I'm just happy you liked it."

She bit her lip then met his green eyes. "But if I don't pay, then I can't wait for you to say 'here's your change.'"

He smiled. Their eyes locked, and if this were a book, this would be the moment the hero realized he was head over heels in love with the heroine. But this wasn't a book... this was real life, and moments like that didn't happen, at least not so quickly.

"Thanks for the drink and the chat." She gave a wave and before she fell victim to the fantasy, she walked away, reminding herself that reality never lived up to her expectations.

# three

Lauren took the spinach and artichoke dip out of the oven and placed it on the counter. The desire to dive in was held at bay as she watched the cheese on top bubble. She was hungry but not enough to scorch her mouth. While she let the dip cool, she cut up cheeses and cured meat to place on the charcuterie board. She didn't even know what a charcuterie board was until Lily May joined book club and brought one over. Ever since then, they switched off who was responsible to make the meat and cheese filled board since it could be a bit expensive. Though, while everyone's was always delicious, Lily May still held the title for the best one.

Lauren arranged the cheeses and meats then added olives, crackers, and some crusty sliced bread to the board. It was like a work of art, and she took a moment to admire it before bringing it over to the coffee table in the living room where they would all meet.

The wine and glasses were next, and by the time Lauren poured her first glass of wine, everyone was sitting in a chair around the coffee table with their book in their lap. Lauren had started book club almost on accident. One day she was sitting on the couch reading, and Olivia, one of her roommates, asked what the book was about. From there Lauren started talking about the story, and by the time she'd finished, Ginny and their other roommate, Ashlynn, had joined. After that they decided to make it a monthly thing where they drank wine, ate finger foods, and talked about books.

Over time new members joined, and they welcomed them with opened arms. Jemma, Steven's sister was one of the newest members and Lily May. Though, Lauren suspected Lily May cared more about the socializing part than she really did about the books. Either way, their little group was the highlight of Lauren's month.

"What did everyone think of the book?" Lauren asked as she settled into her chair with a small plate on her lap, book in one hand and wine glass in the other.

"Loved it!" Lily May exclaimed.

"I thought the girl was annoying," Jemma said, plopping a chip with a healthy scoop of spinach artichoke dip in her mouth.

"I could see that," Lauren added. "But I feel like she was just misguided. She really didn't know any better."

"Still annoying," Jemma said. "Being misguided is one thing; being a complete moron who constantly puts yourself in horrible situations is another."

"I have to go with Jemma on this one," Ashlynn said. "The girl made one bad decision after the next. I started yelling at my book at one point."

"Is that what that was?" Olivia asked before reaching for her glass. "I was wondering if I should go check on you. You know, in case you were being murdered." She took a sip of wine. "But my nails were still wet."

"Gee, thanks." Ashlynn laughed. "Good to know your nails are more important than me being murdered."

Olivia shrugged. "The yelling stopped, so I figured all was good."

"Or I could've just been dead." Ashlynn's voice rose with amused disbelief.

"But you're not," Jemma said.

"But I could've been," Ashlynn argued.

"I… I think a lot of it had to do with her childhood. Her backstory was p…pretty tumultuous," Ginny said. "That could mess anyone up."

"That's what I thought," Lily May said.

Lauren went to defend the girl, then stopped herself before Lauren let the mixed bag of emotions raging inside her get the best of her. A lot of the girl in the book's backstory was her own. Parents who never should have had her, and not only because they weren't ready, and no amount of time would ever had made them ready, but because they were too selfish to put their own wants and needs aside for their own child.

Lauren related to the girl in the book on that level, but unlike the girl, Lauren wasn't misguided. Thank God Grandma and Grandpa had stepped in to raise her when the courts took her away from her drug addicted parents. She could only imagine where she would have wound up if they hadn't. Still, she'd like to think that she would have somehow managed to stay a good person and surround herself with good people.

Lauren mulled over her thoughts for a moment more,

trying to keep her own emotions out of it. "I don't think she can completely blame her upbringing. Plenty of people came from a place like that and turned out fine. I think her problem is she continuously surrounded herself by bad people, and that's why I think she was misguided."

"Which is why she was so annoying," Jemma said. "When her aunt came to help her and she completely blew her off." Jemma rolled her eyes. "I wanted to reach through the book and strangle her. How many people had to reach out to her?"

"She was her own worst enemy," Olivia said.

"Put yourself in her shoes," Lily May said. "She was betrayed by the people who were supposed to love her most. Wouldn't that give you trust issues? Keep you from opening up to someone?"

When Dylan broke up with her, he told her it was because she was emotionally unavailable. That she preferred to keep her nose in a book than have an actual conversation because she was scared it would get too deep.

She thought he was being dramatic, but maybe he wasn't…

No. That was ridiculous. She had put her book down the other night to speak with Gavin. She told him about her pants-wetting incident for heaven's sake. Dylan was just an idiot.

"Like how Lauren was getting all friendly with Gavin the other night?" Lily May said, and Lauren's head snapped up to all eyes focused on her.

"Huh?" Heat spread up her neck through her cheeks

and into her ears. "I was not getting friendly with Gavin."

"Y…you were definitely talking a l…lot," Ginny said, her stutter coming out.

"He's a bartender. It's his job to talk to people."

Lily May shook her head. "It was more than that. Trust me."

"Wasn't Gavin trying to hook up with Rae?" Jemma asked.

"Why don't we get back to the book," Lauren suggested.

"No." Jemma smirked. "I think this conversation is much more interesting."

"Of course you do," Lauren muttered.

Lily May waved her hand at Jemma. "Gavin and Rae met through that dating app, but everyone who has eyes knew that Rae was destined to be with Tommy. Once Gavin saw them together, he knew pretty quickly that it wouldn't be more. They didn't even go on a date. Unless you count her stopping by the bar with Tommy."

"If he looks anything like his brother, then Lauren you should go for it," Olivia said.

Lily May smirked. "He does have good genes and he's totally single."

"I'm not going for anything. I just got out of a relationship, and I'm not ready to date yet. And even if I was, there is no way someone like Gavin would be interested in me."

"Why not?" Lily May asked. "You two would be adorable together."

"Because. He's outgoing and owns a bar. I don't even like leaving the house." Though, she could imagine, lying in bed together, legs in a tangle as she read and he played with her hair.

Lily May tapped a short pink nail against her book. "Semantics."

Lauren threw her hands out, almost spilling her wine, which would have been a travesty. She wheeled herself back in. "Why are we talking about this?"

"Because it's so better entertainment than this book." Jemma held up the book, then let it flop back onto her lap.

"I'm beginning to wonder why you're even in book club," Lauren joked.

"The free food," Jemma said without skipping a beat.

Lily May tilted her head up. "I'm just saying you and Gavin would be adorable together." She gasped. "We could double date. Oh my god, how much fun would that be?"

This was getting out of hand, and Lauren needed to put a stop to it before Lily May took it upon herself to play matchmaker, and embarrass Lauren to the point she never left the house again.

"Gavin is a nice a guy, really nice, but even if he was willing, I'm not ready to jump into anything, so can we please get back to the book."

"Do we have to?" Jemma asked.

Lauren picked up a bowl of chips. "Here have a chip."

Jemma took the bowl and slouched into her chair. "Okay, book it is."

The conversation shifted back to the girl in the book

and why she was the way she was, but Lauren couldn't focus on the story anymore. Her mind was too occupied with thoughts of Gavin Mills and that ridiculously handsome face.

four

It had been five days since Lauren sat at his bar, yet he still couldn't get her off his mind. It was more than the ease of their conversation too. It was the friendly glint in her light brown eyes, the sweet smile that touched her lips when she talked about something that made her happy, and the genuineness of her overall character. After a couple months of failed attempts in the dating world, he'd finally met someone who he wanted to get to know more and who wasn't already secretly attached to someone else. At least he hoped not...

This was the very reason why Gavin found himself heading to the opposite side of the city and walking into one of his brother's apartment buildings.

"Gavin!" Lily May exclaimed, hopping off of the doorman's desk, her tan heels clicking loudly against the tiled floor. Her blonde hair swung with the motion. "What are you doing here?" she asked, hands landing where her cream shirt tucked into the waistband of her light pink skirt.

"I was in the neighborhood and thought I'd stop by."

Lily May's perfectly shaped eyebrow arched. "I didn't just fall off the turnip truck."

"Seriously where do you come up with this stuff? Is there like a southerners handbook that the rest of us folk, don't know about?"

"Hush your mouth and come on up. I need your tallness."

Before he could ask, what she was referring to, she grabbed his arm and tugged him toward the elevator. "Bye, Barney! We'll talk later," she called over her shoulder to the doorman.

"Do you always hang out with your doorman?" Gavin asked.

"Of course," she said matter-of-factly. "He was my first friend when I moved here."

Only Lily May would make friends with a middle-aged man who was paid to monitor the people coming in and out of her building. Gavin was grateful Ashton found a girl whose softness helped smooth out his rough edges.

They went up in the elevator, and she waved him into her apartment before shutting the door. "I need that casserole dish that's all the way on the top shelf and in the back. I was going to grab a chair and do it myself, but since you're here, I figure you might as well be useful."

Lily May was tall especially in her heels, but Gavin had quite a few inches on her. He reached into the cabinet with ease and retrieved the casserole dish she needed.

"Thank you!"

"What are you making?"

"I thought I'd surprise your brother and make chicken parmesan. It's our favorite, and though he always orders out, I figured I'd try and cook it for him. I got a recipe from your dad and just hope I can pull it off."

"I'm sure it'll be great. So listen, I was wondering if you

would happen to have Lauren's number."

The mozzarella and parmesan cheese Lily May just pulled out of the fridge dropped from her hands and landed loudly on the counter. "I knew it!" she exclaimed.

"Knew what?"

"You two totally hit it off the other night just like I suspected you would. Lauren was playing all coy about it, but I knew it!"

"Wait, you spoke to Lauren about me? What did she say?" He felt like he was in middle school, but he was feeling desperate at the moment and didn't quite care.

"Nothing much, but that's probably because I asked her in the middle of book club. She did however get all rosy cheeked when I said your name."

"Did she?" A satisfied smile spread across Gavin's face as he rested against the counter.

Lily May nodded.

"Then why didn't you say anything to me?" he asked. Lily May had been so quick to set him up with every girl she met, so why in the world wouldn't she have come to him with this information sooner?

"You told me not to set you up with anyone anymore, and I was going to ignore you, but Ashton told me to respect your wishes."

Of all the times Ashton could have laid down, this was one of them? His timing really sucked.

"So then I can have her number?"

Lily May tapped a pink nail against her chin. "I don't know. Maybe I should ask her first. I wouldn't like if someone was going around handing out my number to some random."

"I'm not some random. I'm your boyfriend's brother."

"I know that, but to Lauren you're practically a stranger."

She'd opened up to him and told him about her, including how she wet the bed at a fifth-grade sleepover. That had to count for something. "We talked for two hours the other night. We're definitely not strangers."

"Let me just check with her to be on the safe side."

Gavin motioned to her phone, then crossed his arms over his chest.

"You want me to do it right this second?"

"The sooner the better."

"She's at work. They were having a movie night at the library."

"She works at a library?" It made total sense for a bookworm such as herself.

Lily May let out an exaggerated sigh. "You two were talking for almost two hours the other night, and you didn't ask her what she did for a living?"

"Well, no. I didn't think it was important."

Lily May walked over to the fridge and pretended to bang her head against the freezer. "A person spends most of the hours of their day at work; of course it is important. Do you know how much you can learn about a person just by knowing what they do for a living?"

"No, but I have a feeling you're going to tell me."

"You can learn everything about a person. I plan parties

for a living because I'm creative, love people, and I know how to have a good time. Your brother is an entrepreneur because he is driven and determined to prove his worth. You are a bartender because you love people and you care more about social interaction than you do about margins."

"So you have a point."

"I know I do."

"Does being a pain in the ass know-it-all have anything to do with you planning parties?"

"Don't get smart," she said, pointing a finger at him while simultaneously trying not to laugh.

"Sorry."

"Apology accepted; now why don't you tell me what's going on with the bar."

"There's nothing going on with the bar," he said, wondering how the conversation just took this unexpected turn.

Her hands landed on her hips in her signature stance, and she tilted an eyebrow up. "Then why is half of it still under construction?"

"It's not a half, only a quarter."

"Potato patato. Doesn't change the question."

"I hit a minor speed bump."

"Being?" She dragged the end of the word out for emphasis.

"I'd rather not talk about it." The minute he told Lily May, she would tell Ashton and he still wasn't sure he wanted to ask his brother for more money. If he decided Ashton was his last hope, then he would talk to Ashton when he was ready.

"Well, that's fair, but you can either talk to me about it and let me help you, or you can speak to Ashton because he will start bothering you about it. I've been able to hold him off for now, but you know him. It's only a matter of time before he's on your doorstep wanting answers."

Gavin let out a breath and slumped against the counter. Whether he was ready to speak with Ashton, it didn't matter. Ashton had seen the condition of the bar and that wasn't something he would ignore. He would go out of his way to figure out what the holdup was. If Lily May knew the situation, she'd be better able to help Gavin figure out how to handle Ashton, so even though he had reservations, he told her.

She nodded as he spoke, listening intently and continuing to work on her chicken parm dinner.

"So you see," he said. "I'm stuck. Without the funds to do it I'm at a standstill. And if I ask Ashton, I'll owe him even more money than I do. I'll be lucky to even pay him back what I've already borrowed, and he will hold this over my head for the rest of our lives."

"If "ifs" and "buts" were candy and nuts, it would be Christmas every day."

Gavin scratched his head. "That handbook would come in real handy right about now."

"Oh heavens to Betsy! It means stop making excuses and ask your brother."

"Is that what it means? Really?"

"Don't make me hit you with this spatula," she said,

lifting it up and moving toward him.

He held his hands up in surrender. "Okay, okay!"

"You're going to talk to your brother then."

"I'll think about it." He still wasn't sure that's what he wanted. Talking to Ashton would be an easy fix, he'd write him a check and he'd be done with it, but the money would always be a reminder to Gavin that once again he couldn't do something on his own. He didn't want to need Ashton to dig him out of a hole, Gavin was hoping he'd be able to do it himself.

"Stop thinking and just do it. If he would have kept thinking about whatever the heavens he was thinking about, do you think you two would be back on friendly terms again?" Before he could answer, she pushed on. "Absolutely not. It took me to drag him out of this apartment building and surprise him with a visit to your bar to get his head out of his booty. You two waste so much time thinking things over."

"That's not true. If I would have thought over the construction, I could have avoided this."

"Here we go with the excuses again. If you would have taken the time to think it over, you wouldn't have knocked down that wall, and you wouldn't have known about the shoddy wires, putting you and your bar in serious danger. It was a blessing in disguise if you ask me and you shouldn't think of it as anything else."

"I'm sure Ashton won't think of it that way."

Lily May sighed. "Ashton buys buildings for a living. If anyone understands the unexpected nightmares that come with it, it's him."

"You really think so?"

"I know so. Perfect example. I used to have to hit my heater with a hammer to get the dang thing to work. He told me he would look into it. Fast forward two months, and now the entire building's heating system has to be upgraded. One problem can open a door to many more, but you can't focus on that. You have to focus on the problems as they arise, and I can tell you, ignoring it won't make it go away. And quite honestly, I don't like you staying in that building knowing about this, so either you tell Ashton or I will."

He met her eyes with a desperate plea. "You wouldn't."

"You must be outside your mind if you think I wouldn't when your wellbeing is concerned. I'll give you a week to talk to him and in the meantime." She grabbed a bright pink stack of Post-its and scribbled on it with a bedazzled pen. She swiped the paper from the stack and handed it to him. "Here's Lauren's number."

It may have been a consolation prize, but Gavin didn't care. He would take it for whatever it was worth.

"Just so you know. You being a stranger had nothing to do with me not giving you her number. I lied. The truth is Lauren just went through breakup, and I'm not sure she's ready to date."

He already knew this but he was curious why Lily May was willing to change her mind. "Then why are you giving me her number?"

"Because you're a good guy, and Lauren deserves that."

His chest warmed and expanded at her words. "Thank

you, Lily May."

"You can thank me by hiring me as the wedding planner to your wedding."

He froze in place, eyes widening at the crazy talk coming out of her mouth. "Aren't you getting a little ahead of yourself here?"

"Nope. I have a good feeling about you two."

He held the bright pink Post-it up, looking at the number and remembering the brunette who captivated him for an entire evening. "Me too," he said—though marriage was a little much—gave Lily May a kiss on the cheek, and headed out so he could make a phone call.

five

Lauren had a day off from the library and decided to stop by her grandparent's house. The years hadn't been as kind to them as she would like, and her grandmother was currently dealing with severe rheumatoid arthritis, which was weighing heavy on her mind since she could no longer do the things she loved like knitting. Lauren did her best to stop by as often as she could and try to lift her grandmother's spirits. Afterall, everything she had in life was because of her grandparents.

Lauren never thought about what her life would've been if it wasn't for them. Her parents cared more about partying than they did about her, and while it had left an ache in her heart, her grandparents' constant love, devotion, and support helped to ease it.

She let herself in the front door and found her grandmother on the couch, watching her stories. "Hi, Grandma," Lauren said loud enough so she could hear her over the TV.

"Sweetie!" Grandma exclaimed when she realized it was Lauren. Her brown eyes lit up. She quickly paused the TV and held her arms up. Lauren gave her a hug and a kiss on her aging cheek.

"How are you feeling today?" Lauren gave her a once over. She had a little more color in her cheeks than she did last time Lauren had seen her, and there was a little less tension around her eyes.

"Better. The doctor changed my medications."

"Good." It had been a case of trial and error, trying to find the right combination for all her ailments. "When's your next appointment?"

"Next Tuesday."

"Do you need me to drive you?" Lauren was lucky that her job was willing to work with her and make it possible to be there for her grandparents just as they had been there for her.

"Nope, your grandfather will take me."

Lauren nodded, though she liked to be there, since neither one of her grandparents ever relayed the information properly, but it was just for a checkup, so she figured she could miss this one.

"If you change your mind and you need me to go, just call me and let me know."

"Can you stop worrying? Now come. Sit down and tell me about your week."

Gavin immediately popped into her head. She hadn't seen him since the night at the bar, but after the book club chatter, she couldn't stop thinking about him. It was crazy to think she was ready to start dating again. She and Dylan had broken up not even two weeks ago, but Gavin seemed to be infiltrating her thoughts more and more. She blamed Lily May for this. Lauren was perfectly content living her life, being blissfully unaware of how great a couple she and Gavin would make until Lily May had to push the issue.

Now she wondered if he'd lay in bed with her while she read, holding her in his arms while he held his own book above them.

That book he had behind the bar was pretty worn, and she was curious to how many times he had read it. She was too busy looking at him to notice the title, and now she desperately wished she had. Knowing what type of books a person liked could tell a lot about them. Was he a sci-fi kind of guy? Non-fiction? Literary fiction? Thriller? Horror? He did find *The Shinning* comment amusing, so maybe he was a Stephen King fan.

She mentally kicked herself, for not thinking to ask him. Of all the things they could have talked about that was the one subject she could have learned so much. It was also a subject that she would have been able to relate to most, and she wondered if she purposely geared the conversation away from it so Gavin wouldn't learn too much about her.

She imagined them talking about books over a cup of coffee. An excited glow in his eyes as he told her about his favorite books. A smile played at her lips as she thought about those two perfect green eyes.

"What is going on in that pretty little head of yours?" Grandma asked.

Lauren waved her hand as if that would swipe away all thoughts of a green-eyed man. "Nothing. Thinking about one of my books."

"With the way you're looking must be a spicy one."

"It is."

"Well then, what are you waiting for? Break that puppy

out and read it to me."

Lauren had been reading to Grandma since she was a kid. It started with *Clifford the Big Red Dog* and had progressed to more provocative reads. Grandma especially loved the historical romances, and Lauren loved reading them to her, except when she'd compare the intimate scenes to Grandpa. There was only so much Lauren needed to know, and anything relating to her grandfather's man bits was not one of them.

Lauren took out the book and gave a little backstory. Grandma relaxed into the couch and listened. Just like when Lauren read to the kids at the library, she made sure to use different voices for each character and play up the dramatics.

Twenty minutes and a couple chapters later, Grandma stopped her just as the earl and the duchess were about to confess their love for one another. Finally!

"Why do you want me to stop? It's the good part."

"I'm just wondering. Does it make you sad to read all these happily ever afters?"

Lauren met Grandma's brown eyes. "No, why would it?"

"Because you and Dylan broke up."

Lauren shook her head. "It was for the best. Trust me on that."

Grandma smiled, but it was half-hearted; clearly there was something else on her mind.

"What is it?" Lauren asked.

"Nothing."

"Don't nothing me. I can see your lips parting like you

want to say something, but you're holding back."

"Fine. I'm worried."

"About me?" Lauren pointed at herself.

"No about the pope, of course about you."

"But why?"

"Because I'm not getting any younger, and neither is your grandfather. We're not always going to be around, and when I part this earth, I want to know that you're not alone."

"First of all, you're seventy-four. It's not like you're in your nineties and going to die on me tomorrow."

"I feel like I'm ninety with the way my health has been."

"You aren't, and you still have plenty of years left in you. Seventy is the new fifty."

Grandma all but snorted. "I'd kill to go back to fifty. At least then I could open a jar and knit. Get some sexy time in without feeling like I look like an unraveled sheet of cellophane."

Lauren held her hand up to stop the TMI assaulting her ears. "My point is you're not going anywhere. Not yet anyway."

"I will fight death at its door until I know that you are settled."

Lauren smiled at the vision of her seventy-four-year-old grandma sparring off with the grim reaper. "As much as I love that scenario, settling down with someone won't necessarily mean I'm settled. It's the twenty-first century. I don't need a man to make me happy."

"No," Grandma said. "You don't. And I know that you

can find happiness in whatever you do, but I want you to have someone to share that with. All of my greatest accomplishments were that much better because I got to share them with your grandfather. I had my very own cheerleader who rooted for me on the sidelines, waiting and willing to help me reach my dreams. And I know it's an old timey thing, and girls are independent now, but I was independent too you know."

Her grandmother was the first in her family to go to college and graduate; she became a book editor for one of the top publishing companies in the country and then gave it all up to have a family. Lauren didn't want to discount any of her grandmother's accomplishments, but their stories were different.

"I know what you're thinking," Grandma said. "You think I gave up my dreams."

"I…" Lauren had never said it out loud but there was a part of her that always wondered why Grandma walked away from the hard work and dedication she had given to get to where she was.

"It's all right because that's what it appears as, but the truth is, your grandfather didn't want me to quit my job. He wanted me to keep working, but I didn't want to. It was my choice. I loved my job, but I loved my family more, and I was lucky that I was able to stay home."

"Too bad my mom turned out to be a total nightmare."

"Well." Grandma tapped her hand. "Such is life. But before her spiral, I had some of the best years sitting on this very couch and talking to her about her day, braiding her hair and watching her grow before my very eyes. Those are the things I hold onto. And I wonder if you close yourself off to the possibility of a future with a man because of your parents especially your mother."

Lauren arched an eyebrow not exactly sure what Grandma was implying.

"Despite her many faults, you loved her, god how you loved her, and then she abandoned you."

Lauren remembered being a little girl, sitting on Grandma's lap, crying and asking why her mommy didn't want her. A girl that young didn't deserve to know what true heartache felt like. She suppressed the tears pushing to the surface for her younger self and cleared her throat. "Her loss."

"Absolutely." Grandma took her hand and squeezed it tight, and offered her a reassuring smile. "But I know that it hurt and probably still does."

"What does that have to do with me not having a boyfriend?"

"When our hearts are damaged, we do everything in our power to keep from ever feeling like that. I think you have had your heart locked up for so long that you don't even realize it anymore."

"That's ridiculous. I'm not locking anything up."

"Then tell me why didn't it work with Dylan?"

She took a second and thought over the relationship and the final day when it all came to an end. "He didn't like the fact that I read so much. He hated my books." Lauren didn't want to admit that her grandma was right especially since Lauren hadn't seen the truth until now.

"Was it the books? Or the fact that you lost yourself in their pages and would never lose yourself in him."

"I guess it was a little bit of both," she admitted.

"When you read your books, you open your mind to possibilities, do you not?" Grandma asked.

"Of course, that's the best part of starting a book. The anticipation of what's going to happen, discovering the characters and their traits that bring them from point A to point B."

"Exactly. Now take yourself out of the pages; do you have the same anticipation in life? And if not how come? Life can be just as exciting as your books, if you only open yourself up to the possibilities."

Grandma's words hit Lauren deep in the gut. "I was not expecting to be sitting on Dr. Phil's couch when I walked into the house today."

Grandma laughed. "I have been watching a little more of him than usual."

"It shows."

Grandma took her hand and gave it a squeeze. "All I'm saying is you should think about what's holding you back and why."

"If I say I will, can we go back to the book?"

"Hell yes, it was the good part. I don't know why you stopped in the first place."

Lauren let out a loud laugh and shook her head. "You're lucky I love you."

"Luck has nothing to do with it, sweetie. Now read."

A few hours later, Lauren walked out of her grandparent's house and hopped into her car. She finally got to the end of the story and was sad she had to say goodbye. The characters in the books she read, even if she was only with them for a short time, became like friends to her. Grandma would tell her to make her own friends, but Lauren had plenty of friends. At least she thought she did…

Ginny, Olivia and Ashlynn were her friends, but the only reason they were friends was because they were roommates. If they never lived together, would Lauren have gone out of her way to introduce herself? Would she have be willing to make phone calls and plans and keep up the get-togethers if they didn't live under the same roof? Now, she would, but that was only because they were already friends.

Maybe everyone was right. Maybe she needed to put the books down and let life surprise her the same way the plots in the books did. She didn't expect to find a knight and shining armor, and she didn't want that either. Sure, they were fun to read about, but in reality, Lauren just wanted someone who she could be comfortable with whether they were out on a date or staying in and cuddling on the couch. She wanted someone who she could talk to and most of all she wanted someone who would find her reading addiction adorable but who would also be interesting enough to get her to put the book down and be in the moment with him.

She pulled up to her house and put her car in park. As she was reaching for her bag, her cell phone rang. Probably Grandma making sure she got home okay. She took the phone in her hand but didn't recognize the number.

Normally she would have ignored it, but maybe this phone call was a plot twist to her life. She wasn't going to pass it up just in case.

She answered and nearly fell out of her seat when the familiar voice drifted across the line. It was as silky smooth as she remembered it.

"Hi, Lauren, it's Gavin."

Lauren wanted to say hi but she couldn't get her brain and her mouth to get on the same page. What in the world was Gavin Mills doing calling her?

"Are you there?" he asked.

"Uh hi," she finally managed.

"I hope it's okay that I'm calling. I asked Lily May for your number, and in her defense, she really didn't want to give it to me without checking with you first, but I can be very persuasive."

"Did I forget something at the bar?" she asked, wondering why Lily May didn't pick whatever it was up herself and bring it to book club.

"No, at least not that I saw. Are you missing something?"

"No. I… Just trying to figure out why you would call."

There was a moment of silence, and her heart beat rapidly against her chest. She could hear each thump in her ear and couldn't help but wonder if Gavin could hear it too.

"I really enjoyed talking with you the other night," he finally said.

That was completely unexpected. She assumed he was doing his bartenderly duty and that the conversation didn't mean anything beyond that, even though it *was* a nice conversation and she fantasized about it meaning more. "I enjoyed talking with you too," she admitted.

"Really? That's great because I was wondering if you'd want to talk some more. Like go out sometime and talk. Not to pressure you or anything because I wouldn't want to make you feel pressured."

"I would like that."

"If you need time to think about… wait, was that a yes?"

She laughed, loving how unsure of himself he sounded. Gavin Mills was one of the hottest guys she'd ever met, and he was charming to boot. The fact that he was babbling while speaking to her was seriously adorable.

"It was a yes," she confirmed through a smile she couldn't seem to control.

"That's great. How about lunch tomorrow? Say around noon."

"I'll be at work." While she did get a lunchbreak, she'd been using that forty-five minutes to help a senior citizen who was a frequent patron of the library with how to use the Internet. His daughter had moved a few states over, and he wanted to video chat with his grandkids. After she showed him the basics, he had asked Lauren to show him a few more things like Instagram that his granddaughter was a big fan of. Lauren couldn't cancel on Carl, though she believed Carl would understand, but still she didn't want to stand the poor guy up.

"I can't tomorrow," she said. "I have something at

work I can't miss. What about tomorrow night? We can do dinner."

When he didn't answer right away, her stomach knotted. Lunch dates didn't usually carry the potential to go on into the night like a dinner date did, and hopefully he didn't think she was trying to move this along too quickly especially since that was the last thing she wanted.

"I can't," he said, and she deflated.

"No, you're right. Dinner is too much too soon."

"What? No, that's not it. I'm working tomorrow. I pretty much work every night of the week except on Monday's when we're closed. It's just until I can hire someone to help cover the hours."

"Are you telling me that you are the only bartender?"
"For right now. When I bought the place, I couldn't afford to take on any employees. I'm hoping in the next couple of months, but until then, I can't do dinner. Unless you want to bring takeout and sit at the bar and watch me work." He chuckled like it was a joke, though it actually didn't sound all that bad.

She thought about her conversation with Grandma and then just decided to take a chance. "What are you doing right now?" she asked.

"I'm getting ready to open the bar. And since my regulars won't show up for at least another hour, and it's usually dead until then, I'll probably sit on my ass and read my book so I don't have to look at that mess of a wall."

"Then you have twenty minutes to get a few chapters in before I get there."

"You're coming now?" he asked, his voice incredulous.

It was time to claim a life she could only dream of. Normally she would never invite herself anywhere or drive across the city to go talk to some guy at a bar, but hearing Gavin's voice had energized her, filled her with promise and even a hint of an unexpected adventure that she didn't want to pass her by.

She got in her car and clicked her seatbelt into place. "Why the hell not," she said.

"Great, I'll see you soon."

Lauren clicked out of the call and tossed her phone into the bag. Excitement zinged through her just as it did when an edge of your seat moment would happen in the book. It was what Grandma was talking about. A feeling that she never experienced because she assumed it was only meant for the pages.

She had no idea what to expect, but she knew that it was going to be good.

Now that the excitement coursed through her in a frenzy, she wished she'd spent more time outside of her books.

She would.

It was a vow to herself. This was s new leaf turning over. By going to Gavin's, she was proving to herself that she was ready to give the real world a chance. Who knew, maybe Grandma was right. Maybe the world was full of its own surprises, and she just needed to give it a chance.

The drive, though, gave her too much time to think. Maybe she was too forward with Gavin. Maybe she should have let him figure out a better date than practically forcing herself on him at the last minute. He was working, so did he really want her hanging around the bar like some groupie? And did she want to be a groupie? Not really, but she did want to see him, and really that didn't make her a groupie. Or did it…

She did her best to ignore the voice in her head telling her this was a mistake and continued driving toward the bar. She was done listening to that voice. For all she knew, going to see Gavin would be a huge mistake, but for once she wanted to find out instead of assuming.

She'd spent a lot of her life hiding from reality because it was easier than dealing with the fact that her parents didn't love her enough to want her. Her life wasn't a game or anything, but if it was, her parents were winning, by making her feel inferior and unworthy of love. Not that she expected love with Gavin. Oh, god no. That was ridiculous; they just met after all, but if she didn't put herself out there, she would never know.

The bar appeared, and she drove until she found a place to park. She flipped her visor down, checked her makeup, and decided to add a little mascara and lip gloss. Nothing too much, she didn't want to look desperate.

Then with a deep breath, she shed her inhibitions, got out of the car, and sauntered toward the bar.

 *six*

Gavin listened to Devin drone on about his boss and how much he hated the bastard. For what it was worth, the guy did sound like an asshole, but Gavin didn't understand why Devin didn't quit. The job drove him into this stool at least three times a week. Gavin was grateful for the business, but Devin becoming a regular made him family, and Gavin hated to see the man so miserable. Then again, miserable was the only thing he'd ever seen Devin as. He wondered if Devin even knew how to be happy.

He couldn't have been much older than Gavin, mid-thirties at the latest, but he ambled around like he carried seventy years of problems on his back. His black hair was starting to gray at the edges, and the lines around his eyes only seem to get deeper each day. There wasn't much Gavin could do for him except offer an ear to listen, so that's what he did.

"Then the bastard." Devin took a swig of his beer, finishing it off and pushing the empty glass across the bar. "Told me I didn't know what I was doing. And get this." Devin wiped at his mouth with his sleeve, and Gavin took the empty and began to refill it. It was only number four. By number five, he would cut Devin off.

Gavin raised an eyebrow waiting for him to finish, but the door opened, and both of their attention was drawn to the girl in the black tights and black skirt with small white polka dots that flared at her hips.

Lauren had that Jessica Day look that he always found adorable on Zooey Deschanel. She smiled at him and gave a shy wave. She looked sweet and innocent though he imagined with a smile that could knock a guy on his ass, she was anything but.

"Hey," he said, enthusiastically. He motioned toward a stool a few over from Devin. The last thing Gavin wanted was for him to catch her ear. The poor girl wouldn't be able to get out of here fast enough.

She slipped out of her coat, revealing her statuesque frame and looked around for a place to hang it. He hurried out from behind the bar and took the coat from her. "I got this," he said. "Take a seat and get comfortable."

She smiled, her cheeks rounding and turning red. "Thanks."

"Yup. I'll get you a drink as soon as I hang this." He hung the coat on the hooks in the far corner near the dreaded construction area and went back. He slapped his hands against the top of the bar. "What can I get you?"

"I have to get up for work tomorrow and have to drive home, so I'll have a…" She tapped a long, thin finger against the swell of her bottom lip. Her light brown eyes widened, and her teeth slid against her lip. "Do you know what a Roy Roger is?" she asked.

"Do I know what a Roy Roger is?" he repeated, his tone playfully insulted.

"Wasn't he a cowboy?" Devin asked, and Gavin

watched as Lauren stifled a laugh.

"Technically he was a Western actor and singer, but what this beautiful lady is referring to is the drink."

He gave her a wink and watched the red on her cheeks spread to her ears. He grabbed a glass and held it up. "The drink is similar to a Shirley Temple," he explained to Devin. "Except a Shirley Temple is made with ginger ale or Sprite while a Roy Roger is made with cola. Both are equally delicious," he said. "And something I drank as a kid at my dads' parties."

"Your dads' parties, sounds fancy," Lauren said, tugging on her sleeves and adjusting them to sit right on her wrists.

"Not really. They just liked to show off their china." They had more than enough of it. It seemed every year they fell in love with a new pattern, but it made gift buying easy.

"I always wonder what it would be like to have china one day. I mean right now I'm lucky if I even use a plate."

"I've been known to use a paper towel or a box a time or two."

"You too?" Lauren laughed. "I'm glad it's not just me. It's just that fancy plates like the kind that can break by looking at them are so expensive. Why am I going to spend that kind of money on something when I can just make do for little to no cost, and if it breaks, oh well."

"Thank you!" Gavin declared, hands flinging out in front of him. "And when you're finished you can just toss it away. Don't have to wash it. I have been trying to tell my dad's that for years! They can't even serve chips without pulling out all the fancy serveware."

She looked at him eyebrow raised in amusement. "Did they serve you your Roy Rogers in fancy wine glasses?"

"Oh no. Only wine belongs in wine glasses. Roy Rogers would go in double old fashioned glasses."

"That sounds so fancy. I don't even know what that is," Lauren said, tucking a strand of brown hair behind her delicate ear.

Gavin reached for a glass and held it up. "We refer to it as a rock glass or a tumbler. And ready for me to get really nerdy?"

She shimmied on her stool like she was bracing herself. "I'm ready."

"A traditional old fashioned glass holds six to eight ounces, whereas a double can hold between twelve and fourteen."

"Look at that," she said. "I learned something new today."

Gavin took a bow. "You're welcome."

"You're pretty proud of yourself right now, aren't you?" she asked, her cheeks pressing up from her smile.

He lifted his fingers, holding his thumb and pointer apart slightly. "Maybe a little."

"He's a pretty smart guy." Devin pointed his finger at Gavin, managing to put his whole body into it and almost upending the stool.

"I don't doubt it," Lauren said, offering the poor guy a smile.

"He's one of the good ones. There's not many like that

in the world, you know? Like my boss who is the reigning champ of assholes."

"Oh."

"You don't believe me?" he asked. "I bet he has a trophy that says asshole that he polishes every night." He waved his finger in front of his face. "Actually, he probably has some poor sap polish it for him."

The first time Devin came in going on about his boss, Gavin automatically thought it was Ashton since Gavin thought some of the things Devin said could apply. Gavin was relieved when he found out he wasn't. He was also relieved to find out that Ashton was actually a really good boss, at least according to his personal assistant, Alex who stopped in for a drink every now and again, and Gavin had become friends with.

"He sounds terrible," Lauren said. "Why don't you quit?"

Devin lifted his glass and downed the rest of the contents. "Because my mom will never forgive me."

"I'm not following," Lauren said.

"My asshole of a boss is good ol' daddy dear."

Gavin's eyes widened, he was shocked he didn't know that little tidbit, but now that he did, it all made sense. Lauren leaned her chin on her hand with renewed interest. "Tell me more," she said.

"Don't encourage him," Gavin mumbled under his breath, knowing darn well Devin was too oblivious to notice or care.

Lauren turned to him and whispered. "This is better

than any book."

The excitement in her eyes at Devin's misfortune would've been a little alarming, but he knew how much she loved a good story. He'd learned that much from her the first time they chatted.

They listened to Devin rant and rave about his father and how he was basically stuck at the family business in order to keep the peace, but really always wanted to own his own business where he was the boss. For the first time in the year Devin had been taking up space on his barstool, Gavin understood the guy completely. He knew exactly how it felt to be pressured by family to do something you didn't want to do. The only difference was, Gavin stood up for himself, refusing to piggyback on Ashton and be his shadow. Devin was so far in his father's shadow it was as if he didn't even have his own anymore. Gavin had always felt bad for the guy but now that sympathy extended to something more deeply.

"I've about talked your pretty little ear off," Devin said. "I should get going, leave you two to your date."

"I'll call you an Uber," Gavin said.

"Already did." Devin held up his phone and waved it back and forth, his body rocking with the movement. "I just got a notification he's down the road."

"How do you know this is a date?" Lauren asked, wiggling her finger between them.

"I heard him on the phone with you."

"Ah," Lauren said.

Devin slipped into his coat and pulled out his wallet. Gavin held his hand up. "It's on the house tonight."

"Are you sure?" Devin asked.

Gavin really needed the money and giving out freebies was probably the dumbest move he could make right now, but it was the least he could do for the guy. "I'm sure."

Devin shook his hand then turned to Lauren. "He's one of the good ones. Treat him well." And with that Devin headed out of the bar.

"Sorry about that," Gavin said as he gathered up Devin's glass and half-eaten bowl of pretzels.

"What are you sorry about?"

"I'm sure you didn't think you'd be listening to some sad guy's story when I asked you to come here tonight."

"Are you kidding?" she said. "He should think about writing a book. That stuff is fiction gold. The animosity and regrets."

"Don't look too happy over the poor guy's misfortune."

She held her hands over her face, but he could see the red blazing across her cheeks. "Sorry. That was really rude of me. I wouldn't want someone to be excited over my crappy history with my parents."

Gavin's curiosity piqued. "Crappy history?"

She pointed at him. "There you go with that bartender mumbo jumbo."

"You kind of opened the gates there."

"I guess I did." Her lips pressed into a thin line, and the light in her eyes dimmed.

"We don't have to talk about it. The last thing I want is for you to feel awkward or uncomfortable. Maybe in time, after a few more dates, you'll want to tell me."

"A few more dates?" she asked, taking the maraschino cherry out of her drink and plopping it into her mouth. She closed her mouth around the little round fruit. With a flick of her wrist, she detached it and placed the stem on the napkin. "You sound pretty confident about that."

"Maybe not as confident as I am hopeful. Besides, tonight can't really count as a date. You spent more time talking to Devin than you did me."

She placed her elbow on the bar, chin resting on her hand and she tilted her head. "Feeling left out?"

"Maybe a little."

"Then I shall pay you all my attention." She winked at him and nodded to the maraschino cherries. "What does a girl have to do to get an extra cherry?"

"I can take this in so many directions," he said.

"Let's keep it PG."

He pointed to his cheek, how about a peck. His elbow rested on the bar and he leaned toward her. She pressed her hands to the bar and closed the distance, kissing his cheek before lowering herself back down to her stool.

He got a cup and scooped several cherries into it before sliding it across the bar. "Jackpot!" she exclaimed and he laughed.

The door opened and two new customers came in and Gavin greeted them with a nod. "Be right back," he said to Lauren.

"Take your time I have my cherries and am perfectly content." She plopped one in her mouth and hummed as she chewed.

He went to help the customers, falling into an easy conversation that Lauren eventually joined. He gave her a few more cherries, catching glimpses of her smiling and humming as she ate them.

After two drinks the pair paid their bill and headed out into the night. Gavin looked at the time when he realized Lauren was the only person left at the bar and he was surprised to see how much time had gone by.

"Want another Roy Roger?" He motioned to her almost empty glass.

Her teeth slid over her plump bottom lip, and he tried not to focus on the sexy curve of her mouth or the way her eyes smiled more than her lips did.

"I really shouldn't. Have to drive and all, and it's getting late. You should be closing soon."

"I don't close until the last person leaves, and since you're the only person here, that's up to you."

She pushed her glass across the bar asking for another without words, and he quickly went about making her drink.

"Is it usually this quiet this time of the week?"

He shrugged. "They built a sports bar around the corner, and they have a ton of TVs and twofers every weekday until seven. A lot of people have jumped ship especially after I started doing the construction. I still have my regulars like Devin who come in a few times a week and a few other people. Not as many as I'd like, but enough to keep me afloat."

She nodded her head toward the disaster in the corner.

"What's going on with all that? Looks like a big job."

He grabbed a glass and put it under the tap of a local IPA. When the glass was half-full, he pushed the tap back into place and took a sip from the glass. "It's bigger than I expected, going to cost more money to fix, and people don't want to come hangout at a place that looks like it was damaged in an earthquake so…" He shrugged instead of finishing his thought.

"Not to point out the obvious or anything, but in order to make money, you need to have a lot more people in here."

"Is that how it works?" he asked with a laugh. His lips turned down. "I know," he said. "I had all these big plans for St. Patrick's Day, thinking this construction would be done."

"Why can't you still follow through?"

"I wanted to make this place scream St. Patrick's Day, you know be really festive with green four-leaf clover banners and green and gold beads to hand out to customers. Make it an all-day thing with brunch where I served leprechaun mimosas and Irish coffee, and for dinner, corned beef and cabbage with shamrock sours and Irish car bombs. There's a small kitchen in the back, nothing crazy, but big enough to handle that."

"That sounds amazing."

It did sound amazing. Gavin had been thinking about it since the idea of owning the bar became a reality. St. Patrick's Day had always been a favorite holiday of his. It was a day people went out and enjoyed each other's company while sharing a pint. It was a day to raise a glass and sing along to songs while making memories that would stay with a person forever.

"It's basically a fantasy at this point."

Lauren's brow furrowed. "Why?"

"I have two and half weeks until St. Patrick's Day is here and very little money and no employees to speak of." He couldn't afford to make corned beef and cabbage; hell he didn't even know how to make corned beef and cabbage. Though, he thought he could call Dad for a recipe.

"I can help with the decorations," she said and his head snapped up.

"Huh?"

"If you want me to that is. I work at the library, which means I'm always creating displays and helping out with kid classes. I'm pretty crafty with a pair of scissors and some construction paper. Give me some glitter and forget about it. I can make you four-leaf clover banners no problem. I could even make some centerpieces to put on the tables."

"Centerpieces?" He didn't even think about centerpieces. It seemed kind of fancy for the Hole in the Wall, but a little sprucing up couldn't hurt. A centerpiece or two might actually be nice.

"All I'll need is some empty bottles, which I'm assuming you have a lot of and some green paint."

"I couldn't ask you to do that." While it sounded like an interesting idea that could really help give the place some life, he couldn't expect so much from her.

"You're not. I'm offering. Let me worry about the décor, and you focus on the drink menus and specials. You don't have to spend much money to get people in the door. You just need to get word out so they know where to come."

"But what about that mess." He waved his hand to the mess that he despised more and more every day. "I don't want to get sued if someone hurts themselves."

She tapped her finger against her chin. "What about a curtain?"

"A curtain?"

"Yeah a curtain. You can suspend rods from the beams in the ceiling and hang curtains from it. I think that should be enough for people to know to stay away from the area."

"I guess that could work."

"Can I ask the obvious question?"

"Shoot," he said.

"Why don't you ask your brother for the money?"

Gavin ran a hand through his hair, tugging on the short ends. There was no use lying about it or coming up with some lame ass answer. He had a feeling Lauren would see right through his bullshit. He met her light brown eyes and shrugged. "Let's call it a pride thing."

"Okay," she said, and he loved how she didn't try to dig further. "So about those centerpieces."

They sent the next two hours discussing construction paper and glitter.

# seven

The library was Lauren's happy place. The minute she stepped inside, the familiar smell of old paper, an earthy tang with a hint of vanilla and a slight mustiness, filled her nostrils. To her it smelled like heaven and not the actual source of cellulose decay. Such an ugly word for such a glorious scent. A smile immediately pulled at the corner of her mouth as she walked through the first floor, waving to Stacy at the check out desk and going straight to the stairs.

Downstairs was the children area where she worked. Helping to grow young minds through books and sharing with them some of her favorite characters from her own childhood was one of the many reasons she adored her job.

The library was also the place where she found her own salvation as a kid when she was dealing with the fact that her parents abandoned her. Grandma used to take her to the library after school every Tuesday, and Lauren would long for Tuesdays so she could race into the aisles, surround herself with possibilities, and carefully select what friends she wanted to join her for the week. The library gave her a sense of normalcy when everything in her life seemed to have crumbled around her. For that, she would always hold it in her heart with the deepest regard.

Her eyes landed on the display she finished the other day. In yellow cut out letters against a green background, it read *Irish I had More Time to Read.* Next to the words was a leprechaun that Lauren was very proud of, from his red beard to his black boots. And next to that a rainbow extending across the wall and leading the way to a display of green books.

For each green book read in the month of March, the child earned a point, and if they reached four points by the end of the month, they were allowed to pick an item from the treasure chest. She could easily recreate the leprechaun, but she didn't think Gavin would be too keen on the childish decoration even if it was really cute. She would stick to four-leaf clovers and green paper flowers for the centerpieces.

But maybe if he decided to go with the curtain idea, she could turn the curtains into a rainbow. She liked that idea, and she got giddy as she envisioned how she would make it come to life.

Her phone buzzed as soon as she placed her bag down. She fished it out and looked at her screen. A smile bloomed on her face. Speak of the devil.

Just wanted to say hi and hope you have a nice day.

Could he possibly be any sweeter?

She tapped into the box and wrote a reply, then decided to delete and send a blushing emoji instead followed by: *Thanks, you too.*

I also wanted to ask if you were busy tonight.

She wanted to say no. Since the minute she left the bar last night, all she could think about was him. Even when she got home, she had no desire to take out her book and lose herself in some fantasy world because she was doing perfectly fine living in her own. When she closed her eyes, his face was like a welcoming light, guiding her toward a peaceful sleep filled with visions of him and that ridiculously sexy smile. It wasn't a bad way to fall asleep.

Unfortunately, tonight wasn't going to work for her. She typed back.

I can't. After work I go straight to school. I don't get out until after ten.

She was in the process of getting her master's degree so she could get promoted to librarian.

Her phone vibrated within seconds. *Loooong day! I hope I didn't keep you out too late last night.*

Not at all. I had fun. I wish I could have stayed later. She hit send before she could overthink it and delete it. She waited for his text, but it didn't come nearly as quickly as the last. Maybe she shouldn't have said that. She didn't want to come on too strong and ruin any chances that they had. She liked him too much for that.

She debated sending a follow up message, just kidding or something to not look like a stage five clinger, but her phone vibrated.

I wish you could have too. Next time you can stay all night. ☺

Stay all night and a winkey face. Was he insinuating she spend the night? Spending the night was usually code for sex.

She wouldn't mind having sex with Gavin, of course not, he was gorgeous, sweet, funny and she really liked him, but she also didn't want to jump into things too quickly and jeopardize something that she felt could be really special.

She was totally overthinking this, but she couldn't help herself. Her phone vibrated, and she glanced down at the screen. A laugh bubbled out, and she smacked a hand over her face, then whispered an apology to the mom and daughter who swung their gazes in her direction.

Winkey face was kind of a creeper move, huh?

She tapped a reply and hit send. *Maybe a little.*

Thought so after the fact. Just pretend that never happened. I don't want to scare you off.

Lucky for you, I don't scare easily.

Good to know. So if you're busy tonight, what about tomorrow?

I'm free after work.

Great want to stop by the bar then?

Another bar date while you're working?

I know! I'm sorry. I'm working on hiring someone. Come to the bar tomorrow. I have off Mondays. I'll take you for a real dinner then.

Okay.

Can't wait!

She slipped her phone into her bag and sat down at the desk. She had a few things she had to get done today, but in order to do that, she needed to get Gavin off her mind. She closed her eyes and forced him away, then picked up the stack of returned books and got to work.

She took her time, looking at each book, especially the newer ones that she hadn't seen before. She made a note of which ones she'd like to read. She always wanted to be able to make the best suggestions to a child or a parent and did her best to keep up on all the latest releases Children's books were even more of an escape than her romance and thriller books and reminded her of how grateful she was to her grandparents and the way her life turned out thanks to them. "That's my favorite," a little girl with blonde pigtails and a toothless smile said as she pointed at the book Lauren was holding.

Lauren squatted down to her level. "I haven't read this one yet. Can you tell me why it's your favorite?"

The girl bit her lip and nodded. "I like the puppy."

"I like puppies too. My best friend has one and her boyfriend has two!" Lauren held up her fingers to emphasis the two.

"My mom said I can't get a puppy yet because I'm getting a baby sister instead, but I don't want a baby sister. I'd rather have a puppy."

Lauren laughed. She looked up, catching the mom's eyes across the way. She was very pregnant, probably due any day, and she was currently talking to Maggie the librarian. Lauren gave her a wave to let her know she had the little girl taken care of. "Baby sisters can be fun too. You can hug them like you hug a puppy and give them kisses, and eventually you can brush her hair and run around with her."

She shrugged. "I guess."

"Want to come sit with me, and we can read this book together?"

Her lips curved upward, and she nodded, a few wisps of blonde falling free from her braid. Lauren held her hand out. "I'm Lauren. What's your name?"

She slipped her tiny hand into Lauren's. "Ava."

"Well, Ava, it is a pleasure to meet you. Now come on,

let's go read about *Pugsly the Pug Puppy*."

Lauren settled into a chair, and Ava sat next to her. She opened the book and pointed to the words. "Do you want to read, or do you want me to read?"

"You read it!" she announced, then her head snapped to where her mom stood, her braid flopping with the movement. Her mom held her finger over her lips, and Ava mimicked the move, turning back in her seat. "I mean, you read it," she whispered, and Lauren stifled a laugh.

Lauren began to read and lost herself in the adorable story about a puppy.

eight

Gavin wiped down the bar after Brody spilled his beer in the middle of an arm-flailing story. The guy had been in before, and this was the third time he sent a glass flying with his arm gestures. Gavin almost asked him to sit on his hands while he spoke for the safety of the other people in the bar. Though, the guy would probably lose the ability to speak if his hands couldn't move freely with him.

Gavin dumped the rag in a wash bin and picked up a dry one. Brody continued to tell his story, and Gavin checked his phone for any new notifications.

There were no new texts from Lauren, but she was on her way. Gavin tried to occupy his mind while he waited for her to arrive, but he was annoyingly anxious. He wished he could take her out on a real date, but that was the downfall of owning his own business and not having the money to hire on staff. He hoped it was only a temporary thing, and with time the business would earn a profit so he would be able to turn his one man show into a well-oiled team of people he could trust. He would turn this place into the go to spot in the neighborhood. Big screen TVs be damned!

The old bartenders who worked here when Lenny still owned the place had all gotten jobs at the new sports bar around the corner. He knew he couldn't keep them on the payroll, but it still stung that they went to his competition.

He wondered if he asked them back if they would come… then again, he wasn't so sure he wanted them back.

He had a vision for exactly what he wished for his bar, and the old crew didn't quite fit the bill. They were too… self-involved. He once caught Johnny using one of the vodka bottles as a mirror when he was supposed to be making drinks for the packed bar.

Gavin clicked into the two new texts he received. One from Rae and the other from Pops. He shot a text off to Rae without hesitation, then stared at Pops text.

We miss you.

He hadn't been home since before Christmas, and he guessed he felt a bit guilty about that. Granted, he was busy with the bar, but if he was being honest with himself, the real reason he hadn't visited his dads was because he didn't want them to bombard him with a million questions about the bar.

Gavin couldn't lie to them, and the last thing he was for the them to know that he was failing. Not after they'd been so happy when he'd told them about becoming a business owner. The pride and joy in their eyes was something that hit him unexpectedly. Until that moment, he hadn't realized how much he craved their approval with the choices he had made in his life.

Going to work with Ashton at Mills Industries was the obvious no brainer choice to make, and when he turned Ashton down, causing a rift between them, he always wondered if his dads thought he'd made the wrong choice. Seeing their ecstatic reaction when he told them about the bar…well that was something he didn't want to ever take away. The only way he knew how to do that was to avoid them even though it made him feel like a complete and total asshole.

He typed three responses before finally settling on. *Miss you too*. He sent the text off and put his phone down.

His eyes moved to the under-construction area of the bar, and he visualized everything he desired it to be. He had hoped by now that there'd be a ping pong table, a dart board, and a chalkboard occupying that space. He envisioned customers placing friendly wagers and even considered running a tournament or two, but looking at the space now in its unfinished state angered him and left him feeling inadequate as his dream seemed to be fading.

"You look like you're staring at a ghost." Lauren's voice came from behind him. The truth of her words truer than she'd ever know. He *was* staring at a ghost in the form of the dead dreams that never came to be.

"Something like that," he mumbled.

He pushed the negative thoughts from his mind and looked at her with a smile. She was beautiful with her hair hanging down in soft waves and she was wearing one of what he was beginning to realize were her signature skirts. This one bright green, and like the others, flared out from her hips. A bright blue shirt was tucked into the waistband, and a large green gemstone necklace sat above her chest.

"What's that?" he asked, nodding to the large tote bag she was holding with both hands.

Her lips tilted upward as she turned to the bar, hoisted

the tote up, and plopped it on the bar. "Supplies," she said.

"I'm not following."

She laughed and it was sunshine on his cloudy mood. "Stuff to make decorations for the St. Patrick's Day Extravaganza."

"I'm still not sure I can pull it off."

"You can and I'm going to help."

"Dude," Brody the beer spiller said. "Are you having an event here for St. Patrick's Day?"

He hadn't really put much thought into it since his and Lauren's conversation. "Um. Yeah."

"Absolutely!" Lauren looked at Gavin before turning to Brody and continuing. "There will be drink specials, food, tons of people, and karaoke."

"Karaoke?" Gavin exclaimed.

Me and my friends have been trying to figure out what to do. The new place around the corner is having a dart tournament."

If he hadn't started construction, he could've had that too. He could have had a lot of things like groups of people still coming in his bar.

"That sounds fun," Lauren said with a not impressed shrug. "But we'll be having a contest for the best dressed leprechaun. A competition for the cities best Irish soda bread and everyone here gets to taste and be the judge. They'll also be a four-leaf clover hunt."

"A four-leaf what?" Gavin said, scratching his head as a nervous tick started to take over his body. Lauren was promising on all these things he wasn't going to be able to deliver. He didn't even know what a four-leaf clover hunt entailed. And what was she talking about with a best dressed leprechaun contest? Did that mean she expected him to dress up as a leprechaun? Was she going to dress up? What was going on?

Yes, they agreed that she'd work on decorations and he'd come up with some drink specials, but he didn't realize it was going to be more than that. He didn't think it could be more than that. He had no idea if he could even afford half the things she just came up with.

Her eyes landed on him and she bit her lip, a pretty red tinge dotting her neck and cheeks. "I'm sorry," Lauren said, her shoulders slumping into themselves. "I got carried away. I just love doing this kind of stuff. I shouldn't have…"

Only a second ago, her face was bright and cheerful. She was taking charge and she genuinely looked ecstatic. He didn't like that one look at him took that away so quickly. "Now I'm curious about the four-leaf clover hunt."

Her eyes met his and she started to inflate again.

"Yeah, how's that work?" Brody asked.

Her face lit up and she glanced back at Brody. "Come on the seventeenth, and you'll find out." She flashed Brody a smile, and he nodded.

If Lauren had the confidence in him to pull this off then he was going to go all out. He tapped the bar and stood tall. "It'll be a five-dollar cover fee," he said, hoping the cover would at least help him pay for the expense and maybe even get him a profit in the end.

"Awesome! The place around the corner is charging

ten. All right. Me and my friends will be here," Brody declared, holding his beer up again with that same gusto.

"Great!" Lauren said. "See you then."

Brody went back to his beer, and Lauren started digging in her bag. Gavin stared at her like she'd lost her damn mind because her confidence in his ability to make this event happen was questionable.

"What was all that?" he asked as she plopped a stack of green construction paper onto the bar.

"What was what?"

"Don't act all innocent on me. You just created an event out of thin air."

She leaned across the bar, her features turning downward. "I told you I was sorry. Once I get started my imagination just gets away from me and I have a hard time wheeling it in.'""

"Don't apologize," he said. "I still don't think I can make this happen, but…" He shrugged.

She placed her hands on top of the paper and met his gaze. Her eyes softened. "I told you I would help you. We're going to make this the best St. Patrick's Day event this city has ever seen."

"We only have two weeks to pull this off." Not to mention his brother's gala next week. "Where am I going to get a karaoke machine or people to make Irish soda bread?"

"Easy. The library has a karaoke machine they let the employees borrow when it's not being used. I may have already put my name on the list for the weekend of the seventeenth."

He didn't know what to say. Her faith in him was staggering, so he just stared at her in awe.

"My grandma makes the best Irish soda bread. Or she did. With her arthritis, she can't really use a mixer anymore or do a lot of the things she once loved, but she gave me the recipe, and I'm really excited to give it a shot. I have a new oven now too after Ginny almost burnt the house down— that's a fun story, I'll tell you about another time. We can ask our friends to attempt making their own bread, though not Ginny. You can even give it a try. Little friendly competition."

Blush filled her cheeks, and he'd be an idiot to tell her no. "I wouldn't want to disrespect your grandma's recipe with a win."

"Oh! I see how it is. I want a little friendly competition, and you're going cutthroat over here. We'll see come the seventeenth if you're all talk."

Shit. Now he needed to find a recipe. He was going to have to call his dads. They were the only ones he could think of that would be able to help him out with this. He'd worry about that later though; he still had more questions.

"And what about this four-leaf clover hunt?"

"That's going to be the fun one. Everybody who wants to participate will get a card with a clue on it. Each clue will bring them to the next clue. The first person or team to find the four-leaf clover is the winner."

"Where did you even come up with this?"

"It's something we do at the library with the kids, but drunk adults will get just as excited trust me."

"I don't even know what to say. You're turning this into a reality for me." Up until a few moments ago, he had given up almost all hope at being able to pull off a big event in that bar this year. Now Lauren was making it happen. She helped him look beyond his own doubts and visions of failure to make him realize that it was always possible.

"You don't have to say anything. Just help me cut out these clovers." She handed him part of the green stack of construction paper and a pair of scissors. He took the paper from her and realized each piece had a hand stenciled four-leaf clover on it. "For the banner," she said.

"You're pretty amazing, you know that?"

Her teeth slid over her bottom lip, that pretty blush filling her cheeks. She shrugged. "That's what my grandma says."

"Sounds like a smart woman."

"She is."

"Tell me about her," Gavin said as he started to cut the first piece of construction paper. "Is she where you get all your creative talent from?"

"Some. She's a knitter, but like I said, with the arthritis she can't really do that anymore. She can't do a lot of things anymore, which frustrates her, and I can't blame her. She and my grandfather have been married for fifty years, but my grandma has always been fiercely independent. She never waited on my grandpa for anything. If something needed to be done, she would just do it. The arthritis has taken that away from her."

"I'd be frustrated too," Gavin said. "One minute you

are doing everything yourself, and the next you're reliant on someone else. It would be hard to get used to."

"Exactly. She's better, slowly starting to accept the things she can't change, let Grandpa help her, but she still carries that independent air about her, and honestly, I don't think she'll ever shed it. It's a part of who she is."

"I can see you get that from her."

Lauren tilted her head, eyes, staying on the paper as she continued to cut. "Really? And how so? You barely know me."

"When there's a bar filled with people, and you choose to sit in the corner and do your own thing. That shows me you're independent."

"Or that I'm antisocial and hate people."

His eyebrow arched. "Do you?"

She smirked. "No. I don't hate people, and I'm not antisocial per se. More like socially awkward."

"You don't seem socially awkward to me at all."

"Oh, but I can be. Some people have mistaken it as me being a bitch, but honestly, it's just me being awkward and unsure of myself."

"You have nothing to be unsure of," he said. She was smart and kind, laidback and easy to talk to.

She hid her smile with her shoulder. "That's sweet of you to say."

He laughed, rubbing at his chin. "I just made it awkward, didn't I?"

"So awkward."

"Okay, sorry, but I'm not taking it back." He followed

the line of the clover, turning the paper and not the scissor like he'd been taught as a kid. Who knew those lessons would come in handy later in life. "This is kind of relaxing." He leaned against the bar, his shoulders easing as he finished the cutout.

"Isn't it? I love when I have to cut things out. Keeps me busy and occupies my mind enough that I don't get bored or overthink things."

"Do you do that a lot? Overthink things?"

"Socially awkward remember? I overthink everything."

"Is that why you lose yourself in books? You don't have to think about what's going to happen next because it's already predetermined for you?"

"I've never thought about it that way." She was silent for a moment, finishing up the clover she was working on. She made the last snip of the scissor and looked up, meeting his eyes. "Maybe."

She picked up the four-leaf clovers she cut out and retrieved a hole puncher from her bag.

"What's that for?" he asked, nodding to her hand.

"To loop the string through so we can turn these into a banner." She began punching two holes in each corner of the top of the leaf. When she was done, she went in her bag again and pulled out clear string and began to thread the clovers creating a banner. She held it up. "Not bad, huh?"

Not bad at all. "That looks pretty great."

Brody and his friends stood up. "Have a good night," he said. "We'll see you on St. Patty's Day."

Lauren smiled and gave a wave while Gavin gathered

the empty glasses and nice tip.

"See you then."

The door opened, a cool night breeze came in, and Lauren ran her hand up and down her arm.

"You cold?" he asked. "I can get you a sweatshirt from upstairs." He pointed over his shoulder to the door that led to the back staircase.

"Upstairs?" Her head tilted at an adorable angle, brown hair falling over one eye. He thought about reaching across the bar and pushing it back behind her ears—girls loved that shit—but he hesitated, and the moment was lost.

He scratched the back of his head. "I live in the apartment up there."

"Oh! That's convenient. After a good night you can stumble upstairs. Don't even have to get a girl to go very far." Her eyes widened. "I have no idea why I said that." She buried her face in her hands and said something else, but he couldn't hear the words as they mumbled against her hands.

He reached out, taking her soft hands in his and lowering them from her face. "That's better," he said. Her cheeks were a vibrant red, spreading across her nose up the bridge to her forehead. "Want me to go get that sweatshirt now?"

"Nope, my embarrassment has done a nice job of warming me up." She slipped off the stool, grabbed the four-leaf clover banner, and skipped over toward the back wall. She turned around, meeting his gaze. "I thought we could hang this—" A loud squeal came from her mouth just as Gavin yelled.

"Watch out." His hands flung forward as if he had somehow developed telekinesis and could stop her from tripping over a piece of metal sticking out of the floor. Her ankle twisted, and her whole body flung forward.

He ran out from behind the bar, watching it as if it was on slow motion replay. She tried to stop from falling and jolted back, trying to keep her balance, her foot sliding and her ankle twisting again throwing her completely off balance and into a heap of green skirt and blue shirt on the floor.

The right side of her body hit the ground with a thud before he could make it to her. A painful sob spilled from her lips, and panic clawed up his throat.

"Oh my god," he said, kneeling beside her. "Are you okay?" His eyes searched her face for answers. Her face contorted in pain, little wrinkles pulling uncomfortably at the bridge of her nose, the same spot that only moments ago was red with embarrassment. A tear slipped down her cheek, and it completely gutted him.

He swiped his thumb beneath her lid, swiping the tear away. "Where does it hurt?" he asked.

She sniffed. "My ankle."

He took her ankle gently into hand and pulled it onto his lap. It didn't look swollen through her tights. He gently touched it and didn't think it felt inflamed but did an ankle swell that quickly? He wasn't a doctor or an EMT. "I'll get you some ice."

He hurried behind the bar, grabbing a clean rag, and filling it with ice. Out of the corner of his eye he saw Lauren attempt to stand. She let out a high-pitched squeal as she put pressure on it, and like the Flash, he dropped the rag; the sound of ice hitting the floor echoed around them. He was at her side in seconds, scooping her up in his arms before she could fall again. "I got you," he said.

She sucked in a startled breath as she stared at him with those pretty eyes that were now etched with pain.

"Hold on to me," he said.

Their warmth mingled together as she wrapped her arms around his neck and nuzzled her head against his chest. He walked, with her in his arms, to the door and turned the lock.

"You don't close for another couple of hours."

"We're closing early tonight," he said. He turned to the bar and headed to the back door that led to the stairs. He stopped when he was halfway there. "I have an ice pack up in my apartment and a couch for you to sit on. If you prefer a chair or a barstool, you can stay down here, and I'll run up and get the ice pack." He didn't want to bring her up there without permission because the last thing he wanted was for her to feel uncomfortable.

He could feel the heat of her cheeks rise against his chest. "Upstairs will work."

"Upstairs it is then." He turned toward the door, his eyes lingering on the blasted metal that he should have done a better job of blocking off. He'd thought it was bad enough to watch his dreams slip away because of the construction disaster, but now someone was hurt and the only person there was to blame was himself.

He carried her upstairs, cursing himself the entire way.

 *nine*

Lauren never expected to be in Gavin's apartment so quickly especially since they hadn't even technically had a first date, but here she was. Her eyes scanned the surprisingly large open space. Black couches were in the middle of the room around a big screen TV and in between the TV and the couches sat a coffee table with several books scattered across it. She tried to zero in on the titles but, she couldn't make them out from where she was in Gavin's arms. He moved toward the couches, away from the kitchen that was to the far right of the space, and placed her on the soft leather.

She reached over and swiped up the books. They were thick, the binding worn, and while she'd never heard of the author or the title, from the cover she could tell they were science fiction. "You like sci-fi?" she said.

He smirked, taking the book from her hand and sitting beside her. "Love it. There's something about the world building that draws me in. Sometimes even more than the characters."

She swallowed, resisting the urge to fan herself. His words were basically foreplay in her literature loving mind, and she needed to cool down before she combusted.

"Let me get you that ice pack," he said.

"Yes!" she blurted at a much higher decibel than she intended. She cleared her throat trying to play it off. "I mean ice would be good. Thanks."

He handed her the book as he stood, and she skimmed through the pages. She noticed a few highlighted passages and stopped to read them. Most of the highlighted sentences revolved around the descriptions of places and scenery.

Gavin came back with the ice pack and lifted her leg, arranging it on his lap. He wrapped the ice pack in a white towel and placed it onto her ankle. She sucked in a breath as the coolness soaked through her tights and into her skin.

"You okay?" he asked.

"Just cold."

"Let me get you that sweatshirt now."

"No," she said, holding her hand up. "I meant the ice is cold not that I'm cold. She didn't want him to get up. She rather liked being on his couch with her foot in his lap. It felt cozy and like it was exactly where she belonged.

He settled into the cushions, and she held up the book. "What is it about world building you like so much?"

"I don't know. I guess it's seeing beyond what is out there and dreaming about what could be. Like my bar for instance. I started there as a bartender, and I dreamed about owning the place one day and transforming it into my own world. I could see everything in my mind so clearly. Where the ping pong table would go, the dart board, where I would set up more tables and maybe even update the small kitchen to serve your typical bar fare."

"And now you own it."

"I do, but what I realized is those dreams were nothing more than an impossible vision. In these books it's as if the world is real. That the writer somehow transported me from our regular world into their vision. Even though it's impossible, on the pages it's real. I envy the writers now more so than ever."

"It's not impossible," Lauren said. "Your bar can be exactly what you want it to be; you just need to give it time. Rome wasn't built in a day, you know?"

"It wasn't? I could've sworn it was all erected in twenty-four hours."

She swatted the book at his chest. "Smart ass."

"How's your ankle?" he asked, darting his gaze away from her and looking at the spot where the ice pack sat.

"It seems to be better." She turned her foot from side to side. It hurt still, but the pain was manageable for the most part. Reluctantly, she swung her foot off his lap. "I should go actually." It was getting late, and she had work in the morning.

Gavin turned his green eyes on her, and they sparkled under the overhead lighting. "Or you could stay."

She tilted her head. "We haven't even had a real date."

"No, but you have, according to you at least, embarrassed yourself multiple times, stayed out past your bedtime, and we've texted well into the night. I think we're past first dates."

"We haven't even kissed yet," she said as a joke, but when she looked at Gavin, it didn't feel like a joke; it felt more like a door opening to the possibility. "Not that we have to kiss. I was just saying that usually one would kiss someone before they sleep over their place. Because you know—"

Gavin's hand reached out, tucking her hair behind her ear and cupping her cheek. "Kissing sounds nice," he said.

"Uh huh," was all she could manage because looking into those deep green eyes, all thoughts vanished from her mind. The only other thing she could focus on was his lips. Would they be as soft as they looked? And what kind of kisser was he? Slow and gentle or fast and fierce?

He moved closer, the heat of his body practically reaching out and wrapping around her like a comforting embrace. His head tilted, and he moved closer still. She swallowed down the uneasiness that lied in anticipation and helped close the gap between them.

Her eyes slid shut, and the anticipation turned into a flutter of butterflies in her stomach. The wait was becoming too much when his lips brushed gently against hers, a feather of a touch that sent an instant jolt through her entire body. She sucked in a jagged breath of pleasure and thrill as his mouth closed over hers in a sweeping movement.

He parted his mouth and deepened the kiss. Tiny heated swipes of his tongue sent warm chills coursing through her body. His hand rested on the back of her head, holding her close as his fingers laced into the long waves of her hair and bunched into his fist. Fiery sparks lit and exploded as she knotted her hand into his shirt, pulling him closer still.

Their lips synced as the soft gentle tenderness turned into a hurried frenzy of give and take before slowing again to a sweet caress of their mouths.

It was over before it began. His forehead rested against hers as short breaths came in quick succession. His thumb ran across her bottom lip, and she glanced up, catching the vibrant green of his eyes.

"That was wow," he said, the edge of his mouth quirking upward.

"Yeah, butterflies in the stomach, heat coursing through the body, better than fiction wow."

He laughed. "I like your definition better."

"I didn't think it could be like that," she said, not even sure if she was in reality or if she was dreaming. Kisses like that simply didn't exist outside the pages of books. With Dylan it had been nice but nothing to write home about, and she'd kissed other guys before, but this. This wasn't a kiss. This was life changing, body numbing, bliss peaking euphoria.

His fingers skittered up her skin, leaving a trail of goosebumps in its path as he reached for the hair that had fallen in her face. He brushed it out of the way, his finger lingering on the curve of her ear. He kissed her forehead, then stood up.

"What are you doing?" Confusion pulled at the edges of her eyes.

"I want to kiss you again," he said with a half-hearted smile.

"I'm okay with that," she said, hoping she didn't sound like a desperate floozy.

He groaned. "As much as I love hearing that, I know once I start, I'm not going to want to stop, and you have work tomorrow."

"Are you kicking me out?"

He laughed, a loud bellowing bark that echoed through the apartment. "I would never do that, but you're right, we haven't even gone on an official date yet."

"It didn't bother you a few minutes ago when you asked me to stay."

He shrugged. "Now it does. You deserve to be wined and dined."

"I don't care about that stuff honestly." All she cared about right now were his lips back on hers. "I prefer herbal tea and pizza."

"Good to know," he said.

Lauren glanced over at the TV and spotted the time on the cable box. "Is that really the time?" How is it so late already?" She didn't want to leave, but she had no choice. If she was going to be a functioning human being tomorrow, she needed to get home and get to bed.

"Come on," Gavin said. "I'll drive you home."

"No, that's really not necessary." She pushed up from the couch forgetting about her ankle. She winced and quickly sat back down. She took a deep breath. Next time she stood, she was going to do it slower in with less vigor.

"You hurt your driving foot. It would be irresponsible of me to send you on your way."

"I don't want to leave my car. How will I get to work tomorrow?"

"I'll drive your car and call an Uber to bring me back here."

"I couldn't ask you to do that."

He smiled at her, those damn eyes twinkling. "You didn't." He bent down and scooped her into his arms.

The couch disappeared from her back as Gavin stood. "What are you doing?" she asked.

"Giving you a lift."

"I can walk," she said.

"I saw you wince."

"Did not."

He tilted his head. "You're right. My eyes must be playing tricks on me."

She blinked at him, biting her inner cheeks to keep from smirking. "They probably are."

"Humor me. Give it tonight to heal." He bent down, leveling her with the couch. "Grab the ice pack. We'll take it to go."

She grabbed the ice pack and towel off the couch.

"Ready?" he asked.

She nodded. "Hold on tight."

She planned on it.

ten

Gavin rolled out of bed, checking the clock on his nightstand, and rubbed the tiredness from his eyes to make sure he was seeing the red numbers correctly. Eight in the morning was early for someone who didn't go to bed until three. He had been up all night kicking himself for Lauren getting hurt. Lauren had said she was fine, though, and after he dropped her off, she seemed to be doing okay. He had checked her ankle before he left, but with her black tights on he couldn't see much. He had no idea if it was bruised and as far as swelling, he didn't have anything to compare it to. It was why he was getting dressed and heading over to her house. He needed to make sure she was okay.

If she wasn't, he would volunteer to do whatever it was she needed done. If she needed to go grocery shopping or vacuum, he was her man. At least until two when he had to head back to the bar and open up for the day. He really needed to hire an employee to help him especially at times like these. Not that he was expecting anyone else falling in his bar and having to take care of them.

He got in his car by eight thirty-five. Lauren had said she didn't have to be at work until nine-thirty, so he hoped he'd beat her before she left. He followed the directions she gave him last night when he drove her home and fifteen minutes later, he turned onto her street.

He pulled up to the house and threw the car in park. He spotted her car in the driveway, then wondered if he should've called first. It was too late for that unless he wanted to be a creeper and text her from the driveway. He was already here; he was just going to go to the door.

He got out of the car and headed to the front of the house. He walked up the few steps and lifted his hand to knock just as the door flew open. Lauren stood in front of him, long hair pulled back in a ponytail, revealing the soft contour of her face. Her black dress flared at the hips and stopped at her bare knees. She wasn't in her usual tights.

His eyes drifted down, unable to resist a peek, but the porcelain skin melded into a nasty blue and black disaster of angry swirls. Her ankle the size of a golf ball.

"Hey, what are you—"

"Holy shit!" he exclaimed.

"Good morning to you too," she said, leaning against the doorframe while she held the swollen leg off the ground.

"Did it look like this last night?" he asked.

She bit her lip, then nodded. "It's a little more swollen today."

"You can't go to work like that."

"I'm not. I'm actually heading to the doctor. You know just to make sure I didn't do more damage than I think."

"How are you getting there?" he asked.

She held up her keys, and he swiped them out of her hand.

"Hey!"

"Sorry, but there is no way you're driving when your

97

ankle looks like that." He eyed the swollen lump.

"I appreciate your concern, but really I can drive myself." She went to reach for the keys, but he stepped back and held them above her head.

"What is it with guys taking things from me, then holding it out of my reach?"

"I'm sorry does that happen often?"

"Never mind," she said, swiping her hand at the dangling keys. "Can I please have my keys? My appointment is in thirty minutes, and I like to get there early."

"Excuse to sneak in a bit of reading?" he asked.

She reached into her bag and pulled out a book with a man chest on the cover.

"That's a lot of abs," he said.

She smirked. "Jealous?"

He lifted his shirt up and loved the way her eyes widened. He ran his hand over the defined ridges. "Not really."

"That's just not fair," she said.

"What's that?"

"You look like that." She circled her finger around his face. "And have abs like that. It's just wrong." He stared at her, and her shoulders slumped. "Why are you looking at me like that?"

"I'm trying to figure out if you think my abs are a bad thing."

"No, of course not." Her eyes drifted to the ground. "It's just not fair. You think they would have distributed the good genes a little to the rest of us common folk."

"You are anything but common. Have you ever looked in a mirror?"

Her attention snapped to him, then she shook her head. "I don't have time for your charm. I have an appointment to get to."

He turned around and bent down in front of her.

"What are you doing?" she asked.

"Giving you a lift." It was the least he could do. Besides, he'd seen the tight set of her jaw and the uncomfortable gleam in her eyes. She might have been trying to put on a front, but there was a slight crack in her façade and he was seeing right through it.

"I am not getting on your back," she scoffed.

"Why not?" He was bent down, ready and willing, all she had to do was jump on.

"First off, I'm in a skirt."

"I won't try to cop a feel, scouts honor," he said, turning to her and holding up his fingers.

"You were a Boy Scout?" She shook her head and lifted her hand up. "Not important."

He loved how fluttered she was getting. "I'm waiting," he said, still bent over in front of her.

She sighed extra loud. "Are you always this insistent?"

"Are you always this stubborn?"

She crossed her arms over her chest, and he admired her resolve. He stood up and turned around to face her without craning his neck. "Fine, you can walk, but I'm still driving."

Her lips pressed into a thin line, and he couldn't help

but laugh. "It's really killing you that I want to help you, huh?"

"I'm used to doing things on my own is all."

As someone who wanted to step outside of his brother's footsteps and do his own thing by himself, it was something he could understand. "I can respect that."

"Thank you."

"But I'm still driving."

She rolled her eyes. "Of course you are."

He held his hand out to signal for her to go. Those light brown eyes of hers looked at him with disdain before settling into a determined stare. She pushed off the doorframe and put her bad ankle down. She barely put pressure on it as she quickly jumped back to the other foot. She did this three times, and he let her, even though he really wanted to scoop her up in his arms.

She got to the edge of the stairs, and she held onto the banister as she hobbled down. All she had to do was say the word, and she'd be in his arms, saving her the pain. He followed behind her, slowly.

"If you don't hurry it along, you're going to be late to your appointment," he said, unable to help himself.

"I would've already been to my car if someone didn't bend over in front of me, blocking my path."

"You're not a morning person, are you?" he asked.

She ignored him and continued on, finally making it to the last step. She stopped, looking from where they were to her car. Her shoulders slumped forward. Enough was enough. He walked over to her and lifted her into his arms.

The scent of vanilla surrounded him, and he swallowed down the desire to bury his head in the crook of her neck.

"I told you I could walk," she said as she wrapped her arms around his neck.

"I know, but you also don't want to be late for your appointment, so I made an executive decision."

"Is that what you're calling it?" she asked.

He nodded. "I'm parked behind you, so we'll take my car."

"You really don't have to drive me."

"And you really don't have to argue with me, but that doesn't stop you."

She closed her eyes and took a deep breath, her chest rising and falling. "I'm sorry," she said, looking up to meet his eyes. "I'm used to doing things for myself. I'm not used to people going out of their way to help me."

"Probably because you don't let them."

"You may have a point there. It's just that"—she shook her head—"Never mind. It's not important."

The tight set of her eyes told him differently, but he understood wanting to keep things to yourself. She would open up to him in her own time. The last thing he wanted was to push her. Right now, the only thing that mattered was getting her to the doctor and making sure she was okay.

He walked them the rest of the way to his car, opened the door, and set her in the seat. When he reached for the seatbelt, their hands touched. His gaze lowered and met her eyes. "Hi," he said.

"Hi."

And because he'd been holding back long enough, he leaned in. His lips brushed hers for the briefest of seconds, but that explosive spark that wracked his body last night when she was in his arms ignited again.

He controlled his urges and stood up. "Please make sure all body parts are inside of the door and away from any exits."

She laughed. "All clear."

He shut the door, hurried around to the driver side, and slid into the driver seat. He loved how his car already smelled like Lauren.

"Let's go get that ankle taken care of," he said.

"Gavin?" she said, her voice a mere whisper.

"Yeah?"

"Thank you."

The sincerity of those two single words reached into his chest and wrapped around his heart. But he didn't deserve that. "It's the least I can do," he said. After all, it was his fault.

eleven

The doctor's office was busy, but Lauren and Gavin managed to find two open seats in a secluded corner of the waiting room. Lauren had refused to let Gavin carry her into the doctor's office even though he insisted, finally settling on wrapping a secure arm around her waist while she made her trek.

She glanced over at him; his hands rested on his knees, and he rocked slightly back and forth. His fingers tapped an impatient beat.

Lauren appreciated Gavin being there for her, she really did, it was just hard for her to accept help. While her grandparents had been there for her growing up, she was fiercely independent and had been used to fending for herself. Allowing someone to help her meant she had to open herself up, and that wasn't something she was comfortable doing.

Grandma was right. Her parents abandoning her had affected her more than she'd ever realized. Dylan had tried in the beginning to get her to open up, but she didn't feel comfortable discussing her family drama, and if she were being completely honest with herself, she was embarrassed that her parents cared more for themselves than their own daughter. Not exactly the kind of thing you want to admit to your boyfriend.

Dylan wasn't the easiest person to confide in either. He could be extremely judgmental, and maybe deep down she thought he would dump her if he knew she was a product of selfish parents, so she shut him down time and again until Dylan gave up, opting to bury his nose in his cell phone rather than keep trying.

That was the difference between Gavin and Dylan. Gavin was open-minded and determined, the type of guy that wouldn't give up so easily. But what if she pushed him away too? And he got fed up with her. They hadn't even gone on their first date yet, but she was already afraid of losing him.

He took her out of the pages and showed her that life could be just as swoon worthy as her favorite books, that kisses could make a million sensations course through her body, and that falling head over heels in love was possible. She knew falling in love with Gavin was far off, but she could see herself falling down that endless abyss the more time she spent with him.

But what if she lost him before she got the chance to fall?

"My grandparents raised me," she said, and his fingers came to a stop on his jeans, his leg stilled. He turned to look at her. She swallowed, finding the courage in his quiet assurance. "The reason they raised me was because my parents abandoned me. They were more concerned with getting their next fix than having a daughter to take care of. When I was five, they left me at home and went on an all-night binger. The neighbor heard me crying and called the cops. I got taken away from them, and instead of trying to clean up to get me back, they just took off. My grandparents found out I was in foster care and fought to get custody. Without them, I don't know where I would be today. What my life would be like. I owe them everything. But because of my parents, because they abandoned me, I have a hard time opening up to people, which you might find surprising since I just word vomited all over you."

Gavin sat there, staring at her, not a peep coming from his mouth. She shifted uncomfortably in her seat. Instead of not opening up enough, she did the opposite, completely drowning him in her baggage. She was surprised he hadn't bolted out the door, leaving her in his dust.

"I have no idea why I told you all that," she said, trying to at least end the awkward silence.

He took her hand and brought it to his lips, pressing a kiss to her knuckles. "I'm happy you did."

"Really? Because you didn't say anything."

"Honestly, I was taking it all in and realizing." His eyes crashed into hers with an intensity that made her breath catch. "How incredibly brave you are."

She shook her head, needing to put a stop to that train of thought immediately. "I'm not brave."

"You are. You're so brave you can't even see it in yourself."

"I had my grandparents. I was lucky, unlike so many other kids. Those are the kids who are brave. The kids that get bounced around from one foster home to the next."

"Your situations are different, and yes you are lucky to

have your grandparents, but some people let the trauma of their past define them. Not you."

"I do though. I close myself off and won't let anyone in."

He turned in the seat to face her completely and gently pushed her hair behind her ear. She blinked up, meeting the deep green of his eyes. "You just let me in."

A smile spread across her face. "I did, didn't I?"

He nodded. "You did. I'm proud of you."

She shrugged. "Thanks." She pointed a finger at him. "But don't expect that all the time."

"I wouldn't even think it." He laughed.

"Now what about you?" she asked. "Any deep-rooted emotional baggage you want to share with the class?" He was quiet for a moment, and from the pucker of his cheek she could tell he was nibbling on the inside. His lips parted as his eyes met hers.

"Lauren Logan."

His mouth snapped shut, and he turned away.

"Lauren Last Name," the nurse called from the door.

"Here!" Lauren said, holding her hand up. She looked at Gavin, mad that they didn't get a chance to finish their conversation. "I'll be back," she said. "Don't have too much fun without me."

He got up from his chair and held his arm out. "I won't, but at least let me help you to the door."

She latched on and leaned her weight on him and they made their way to the nurse who was patiently waiting.

"Go get em' Tiger," he said as she hobbled away.

***

Gavin sat back down and tried to occupy his mind, but all he could think about was Lauren's ankle. The swelling was ugly, and the guilt was eating at him. He reached into his pocket and took out his cell. He clicked into his contacts and scrolled to Ashton's name. His finger hovered over the name. All he had to do was hit call, step outside, and have a conversation with his brother, it shouldn't be so hard.

It was just money nothing more. But no matter how many times he repeated that thought, he knew it was a lie. It was so much more than money. It was admitting to failure, giving Ashton the pleasure of saying I told you so.

When Gavin had gone to Ashton a few months ago for the loan, Ashton had originally told him no and that he was saving Gavin from a life of debt. *Saving.* Like Gavin was some helpless dimwit who couldn't do anything without his brother's help. It had pissed him off and pushed him to the point of honesty. That honesty was what changed Ashton's mind. Gavin had every intention of paying every single penny back with the added interest, if he didn't pay it back in time of the parameters they'd set up. He was a man of his word, and he didn't care if he paid that last cent back with his dying breath, he would pay it.

Gavin loved Ashton; he was his twin, partner in crime all through their childhood, but Gavin didn't want to piggyback off of Ashton's success. This bar was his way of carving his own path in the world, and he couldn't even do that himself. How was he supposed to know that opening up a wall would open a pitfall full of problems?

He dropped his phone in his lap, ran his hands through his hair, tugging on the short ends before resting his hands on his knees. His legs shook with nervous energy.

Twenty minutes had passed, and Lauren still hadn't come out. He hoped she didn't have to get x-rays. That would just be the icing on the cake if it was more than a swollen ankle.

He couldn't just sit there, so he got up and walked over to the window. The receptionist was an older woman with short salt and pepper hair. She glanced up at him over her red rimmed glasses. "How can I help you?" she asked.

"My friend is back there, and I wanted to pay her copay."

"That's very kind of you."

He reached into his pocket and pulled out his wallet. He didn't exactly have the extra funds, but he couldn't have Lauren paying for something that was his fault. The least he could do was cover the cost of her appointment. He handed the woman his debit card and waited for her to finish the transaction.

She handed it back and gave him the receipt. "Thanks," he said and was about to head back to his seat, but the door opened, and Lauren came out on crutches.

His eyes widened, heart stuttering to a stop. "Please tell me it's not broken," he said.

Long lashes blinked up at him. "Not broken, just really swollen. The doctor said I should keep weight off of it for a few days, continue to ice it, and he gave me this," she said, holding up a small piece of paper.

"Paper how nice of him."

"It's a prescription for pain meds, you dope." She smiled, then her eyes cast down. "I doubt I'll fill it though."

"Why not? If it'll help with the pain."

"I told you about my parents." She glanced up. "I don't want to ever wind up like them."

Gavin took the script from her hand. "That'll never happen."

"Addiction clearly runs in my blood."

"Why don't we get you home. You can see how bad the pain is and decide then."

"I'd like that."

"Good let's get out of here."

"I have to pay first." She turned on her crutches. "I'll just be a sec."

"It's already taken care of."

She turned around, upper body, resting on the crutched. "What do you mean it's taken care of?"

"I took care of it." He held his hand up. "And before you get your panties in a bunch, I get it, but I'm the reason you're here, so just let me have this one."

"My panties are not in a bunch."

"I think they are."

"Maybe if I was wearing some," she said, leaving him with his mouth open as she swung herself past him on her crutches.

twelve

"Do you need anything else?" Gavin asked as he stood at the head of her bed. He already went to the pharmacy and filled her prescription just in case, got her extra blankets from the hall closet, propped her foot on top of a pillow, stacked a pile of books on her nightstand, made sure her Kindle and cell phone were fully charged, and made her a hot cop of apple cinnamon tea.

"I'm good," she said, unable to prevent the smile spreading wide across her face. "I've been good since you made me brunch in bed." He only microwaved a prepackaged egg sandwich Olivia had bought, but it was the thought that counted, and there was definitely a lot of thought behind it. "You should go."

"I feel bad leaving you here alone."

"It'll only be for a few hours before Ashlynn gets home, and Ginny is right across the street if I need her. I'll send her a text."

"I'll take care of it. I'll stop over there when I head out."

"I let you help me with a few things, and now you're taking over," she said with a laugh.

"Only while you're down for the count."

He walked over to her and bent down, giving her a sweet kiss. "Text me if you need anything."

"And what? You're going to close the bar up and come over here?" She fluttered her eyelashes. "I'll be fine."

"If I have to close my bar, I will."

"It's just a swollen ankle, Gavin." She hated to see the concern that had been tightening the skin around his eyes from the moment he arrived that morning. She wanted to kiss it away and watch him relax back into the laidback guy she knew.

"I'll call you later." He turned to walk away, and Lauren grabbed his hand. He looked back at her, his eyebrows drawn together.

"It's not your fault, okay? So stop blaming yourself."

"I'm not," he said, but it was a pathetic attempt at a lie.

"You are, and you're making me feel guilty about it, so stop. It wasn't your fault. I should've been paying attention because I knew that area was under construction. It was a stupid accident because of my own carelessness."

"What if you fell and hit your head?"

"I didn't. I twisted my ankle. The doctor said I'll be fine in a week."

"It shouldn't have happened."

His eyes lingered on their fingers as she laced them together. "Stop being stubborn and look at me," she said.

"I thought we established you're the stubborn one." He lifted his gaze; that sparkle she loved was back, even if for only a second before it dulled again.

"It appears you can be just as stubborn."

"I don't like seeing you in pain."

"And I don't like seeing you looking like someone stole

your puppy."

"What kind of monster would steal a puppy?" His stoic resolve cracked and he smiled.

She poked at his side. "Was that a smile?"

He tried to cover it with his hand but started laughing.

"Are you laughing?" she asked.

"What can I say? I've been making myself laugh since the nineties."

"Okay, old man."

He gasped, holding a hand against his chest. "Old man? That's hurtful."

"They say the truth hurts sometimes."

"I didn't realize you had an evil side."

"Stick around. There's a lot you don't know."

He looked at the clock on her nightstand. "Crap. I really have to go. You sure you don't need anything else?"

"Positive! Now go. Please."

"Enjoy your book," he said, kissed her forehead, and took off.

Lauren settled into the soft warmth of the pillow fort Gavin made around her and picked up her newest read, a dystopian with a kickass female lead. After spending so much time in reality, she was ready to slip back into the world of fiction.

Though as she started reading, she couldn't help but picture herself as the female main character and Gavin as the romantic lead. Mixing reality with fiction had never been so fun.

**

Gavin hurried across the street and knocked on Ginny's door. A round of barking greeted him, and Ginny appeared a few seconds later. She ordered the dogs back as she flipped her hair into place and slipped out the door. She pulled it shut behind her, the sound of nails scratching on the wood.

"Hey, Gavin," she said. "W…What are you doing here?"

"Sorry to bother you."

"No, no bother."

He tossed a thumb over his shoulder. "I was at Lauren's. She hurt her ankle, and the doctor told her to keep off of it. I have to head to the bar, and I feel bad leaving her alone, so I was hoping you can check on her in an hour or so."

"Absolutely. Is she okay?"

"She will be. She took a tumble last night at the bar. Tripped on a piece of metal sticking out of the floor and twisted her ankle pretty good."

"Oh no!" Ginny's hand landed on her open mouth, making Gavin feel even worse than he already did.

"I would stay, but I have to open the bar," he said, feeling like he needed to justify why he was leaving her alone and injured.

"Of course and I'm sure Lauren wants you to. She's not exactly the type that likes to be fussed over."

That was the understatement of the year. "You're telling me. She fought me all day from the car to the doctor's office to the pharmacy and back."

"Y…you went to the doctor with her?" Ginny asked,

tucking a green strand of hair behind her ear.

"I didn't exactly give her a choice."

Ginny smiled. "Good."

His eyebrow arched in curiosity. "Good?"

"When she had the flu, she wouldn't let me or Dylan take her to the doctor. She went by herself."

What kind of dip shit would let their girlfriend get behind the wheel when they were battling the flu? Did he even try? Gavin wouldn't only have refused, he would have made sure she had everything she needed.

"Explains why he's not around anymore," Gavin said.

"One of the reasons."

"What were the others?" Gavin knew he shouldn't ask, it was none of his business, but he couldn't help himself. Lauren was a complex woman that he really liked, and he wanted to understand her better.

"It was like a whole bunch of little things that accumulated into the simple fact that they didn't belong together. I saw you two at the bar, and she never looked up long enough from her book to look at Dylan the way she looked at you." Ginny shrugged. "But y…you d…didn't hear that from me."

Gavin held his hand over his heart. "Your secret is safe with me." Gavin glanced up and spotted three dogs in the window, fighting for prime view.

"Your dogs are waiting for you," Gavin said. "I won't keep you any longer." He stepped back. "Thanks Ginny."

She smiled. "You're welcome."

Gavin got in his car and looked at Lauren's house. His

lips quirked as he remembered standing in front of her bent over while she stubbornly stood in the doorway. She had been so cranky this morning.

He had a feeling that hiding who she truly was had become her own personal crutch, and he loved that she didn't hide her true colors from him.

Happy or cranky, he would take her anyway he could get her.

He put his car in reverse and reluctantly headed back to the bar.

thirteen

It was another quiet night with a handful of customers, and Gavin was starting to worry about making enough money to keep the place afloat. He had a few customers in but nowhere near the capacity he needed to pay all the bills. He needed to think of something and fast, or he'd be either closing up shop or asking Ashton for help.

"I'll take one more," Devin said, and Gavin grabbed his empty glass to refill it. He turned to the taps and pulled down on the pilsner, filling it to the brim. He pushed the glass across the bar and went to the register.

"Gavin Alexander Mills!" Lily May's voice boomed across the bar.

Gavin flopped his rag over his shoulder and turned to the door along with every other pair of eyes in the bar.

Lily May was wrapped in a green corset covered in ivy leaves and a matching pair of the tiniest green shorts—if you could even call them shorts—and a bright red wig that matched her lipstick fell in curls down her back. Leaves replaced her eyebrows, framing her blue eyes, while green tights with twisting ivy covered her legs. The ivy continued in a single vine around her arm. She stood tall in green high heels, her hand planted firmly on her hip.

"Hey!" Gavin yelled at the men who were drooling at her. She and Ashton had only been dating a couple months, but he'd already considered her like a sister, and he would not hesitate to defend her honor if it came to that. "Divert your eyes, boys," he said, and the sound of butts turning on stools and chairs interrupted the silence.

Gavin pointed a finger and twirled it at Lily May. "Spend your day being one with the trees or something? I know you miss North Carolina but this is a bit much."

"If you don't stop talking, I'll tear your arm off and beat you to death with the bloody stump."

His lips pressed into a thin line, trying to control his laughter. "Violent."

"I am madder than a wet hen, and I don't need you trying to be funny."

"What'd I do?"

"What'd you do? Poor Lauren is hobbling around because she hurt herself in your bar!"

Gavin waved his hand to Lily May to quiet her down; he didn't need his customers to hear about an injury in his bar. He didn't want them getting any ideas.

"I know," he said. "And I feel really guilty about it. I went with her to the doctor to make sure everything was okay and paid her copays."

"And have you talked to your brother yet?"

"No."

"Why the heck not?"

Gavin went to speak, but the words stuttered on his tongue because he didn't have a rebuttal. He had no reason other than his pride standing in his way like it always did. "Haven't gotten around to it."

"Oh heaven's to Betsy! That is the saddest excuse I have ever heard, and I have heard some pretty pathetic ones in my day. You either talk with him today, or I will."

He could stand here and argue with Lily May until he was blue in the face, but she wouldn't budge, and she shouldn't have to. Gavin was being an idiot, and he needed to get over himself and do the right thing for him, for the bar, and for Lauren. If he would have spoken to Ashton in the first place, she never would've gotten hurt. The only person to blame was himself.

"I'll talk to him."

"Good!"

"Now do you want to tell me why you're dressed like Poison Ivy in the middle of the week?"

"I was at Ginny's house trying on my costume for the next comic convention when I saw Lauren and she told me what happened. I grabbed my purse and came right here."

"You could have just called."

"Sometimes in order to get things done you simply have to do them in person."

"Even if you're dressed like you just stepped off the pages of a comic book."

Her lips tilted up, eyes growing wide. "Really? You think I look like I just walked off the pages of a comic book?"

"Absolutely."

"That is the best thing anyone has ever said to me."

"Don't tell Ashton. He might get jealous."

Lily May waved her hand. "Oh, knock it off. Don't ruin

this moment for me. I was worried I didn't get down the ivy just right."

"I'd say it's pretty perfect."

She let out a squeal, and all eyes were back on her. Gavin narrowed his gaze on everyone, and they turned back in their seats.

"You should go and put some clothes on. If Ashton were to walk in here right now, he'd have a heart attack with the amount of skin you're showing."

"And I would tell him he needs to get over it. I am wearing this to the convention whether he likes it or not. Besides all these men can stare all they want. At the end of the day there's only one man I care about, and he should be home soon. I think I'll go surprise him."

"Oh, he'll be surprised all right."

She held her finger up and pointed it at him with gusto. "Don't you go texting him."

Gavin lifted his hands in front of him. "My mouth is sealed."

"Unless you want to tell him about your little problem."

"I'll take care of it."

He just needed to find the right words, and, Ashton, I messed up wasn't exactly sitting well with him at the moment.

Lily May headed for the door, and a lightbulb exploded in Gavin's head. "Hey, Lily May." She spun around on her heels.

"I'm going to do a St. Patrick's Day thing here at the bar, and I was wondering if you'd—"

"I'm in."

"You didn't even hear me out."

"Lauren already told me. I was surprised as all get out that you didn't come to me first. To be honest it really dilled my pickle."

"I knew you were busy with the gala."

"I've been done planning that for weeks now. I'm just sitting around waiting for the big event. Besides, it'll all be over come next week, and then I'll be free for a bit before I start a new project."

"I don't know if I can afford you," Gavin said. Lily May charged a pretty penny for her services.

She waved her hand. "You can pay me by getting all that fixed and taking Lauren to the gala."

"What? I'm taking Rae. I told you that."

"I know, but I invited Tommy, so that would be an awkward threesome if you ask me."

"That's probably why she called," Gavin said, remembering the missed call on his cell earlier in the day when he was doing inventory.

"Both your names will be on the list. I'll call you to go over the St. Patrick's Day stuff tomorrow. See you later." Lily May gave one final wave, her red wig trailing behind her as she disappeared out the door. Gavin turned back to his customers, who were all staring after Lily May. He snapped his fingers, and they all turned back, acting as if they weren't just ogling her.

He shook his head and refilled drinks while going over what exactly he was going to say to Ashton.

fourteen

Lauren would always kill for an excuse to stay in bed and read all day, but now given the chance, reading was the last thing she felt like doing. None of the heroes interested her at the moment. She preferred a particular green-eyed bartender who made her laugh.

God, she was becoming like the heroines in her books, and she didn't care. She rather enjoyed the idea of having someone to think about and wonder if he was thinking about her too. It wasn't like that with Dylan. She didn't care what he was doing or when she'd see him again. She'd actually get annoyed when she had to put down a book to meet up with him for a dinner date. How she didn't realize then that they weren't a match made in heaven was beyond her.

She wasn't even sure if she got hurt if he'd show up to make sure she was okay like Gavin did. Maybe Dylan would have sent a text, maybe even a call if he was feeling particularly worried, but he wouldn't just show up unannounced to take care of her.

Her phone beeped, and she grabbed it off the nightstand. A warm giddy feeling filled her up at Gavin's name on her screen. She clicked into the text.

Just checking in. Want to make sure you're okay.

She typed back.

We're fresh out of mint chocolate chip ice cream. Other than that,

I'm good.

Mint chocolate chip, really?

Her eyes widened in playful shock, and her mouth fell open. *It's only the best flavor.*

It tastes like toothpaste.

Take that back!

Seriously I feel like I should get my toothbrush when I'm eating it.

There is something wrong with your taste buds because it's the best!

I think it's the other way around.

Let me guess your favorite flavor is she tapped her lip as she thought. *Vanilla.*

There is nothing vanilla about me ☺

Heat rushed into Lauren's cheeks as she tried to think of something witty to say in reply. Before she could dazzle Gavin with her quick wit, her phone beeped. She looked down at the new text bubble.

I'm sorry. I would go get you ice cream if I could, but I have customers.

She shook her head as if he could see her. *I wouldn't expect you to drop everything and come get me ice cream.*

Just know I would if I could.

Yup, nothing vanilla about you all right.

He sent back a simple *lol,* and she put her phone back on the nightstand. She picked up her book and tried to read again. Finally, she slipped back into the world and engrossed herself in the characters. The pages flew by, chapter after chapter as she sunk further and further into the fantasy. She had no idea how much time had passed. When she was reading; time was as inconsequential as an umbrella without rain.

Just as the heroine was about to steal a horse, there was a tap at her door. She held her finger up, finishing the paragraph she was on then glanced up.

"Have I ever told you how cute you are with those glasses on?" Gavin asked from the doorway, and her eyes widened in surprise. He leaned against the frame, arms behind his back, green eyes looking down at her.

She looked at the clock sure it had to be well past midnight, but it was only nine.

"Olivia let me in. I hope that's okay."

"What are you doing here? The bar doesn't close for a few more hours."

He pulled his hand from behind his back and held up a tub of mint chocolate chip ice cream. "You needed ice cream," he said.

She stared at him shocked and amazed at this sexy man who was more thoughtful than any guy she'd ever known other than her grandfather that is.

"What about the bar?"

"I closed early. The group that had been here left, and no one new came in so I turned the sign. I'd rather spend the rest of the night watching you eat toothpaste ice cream than sitting alone in the bar just in case a straggler stumbled in."

The bar was his livelihood, and he closed it early for her. She didn't want to get ahead of herself and think too far into it, but that felt pretty damn great.

Something had always held her back from connecting to Dylan on a different level, an intimate level. For some reason it had scared her to cut herself open and let someone peer inside, but each second she spent with Gavin, the closer she became to being okay with the idea of letting him in.

"You didn't have to do that," she said. "But I'm happy you did."

He smiled. "So can I come in, or do I have to spend the rest of the night holding this doorframe up?"

She laughed. "Do you have a spoon?"

He pulled one out of his pocket and held it up. "I'm always prepared."

She adjusted herself on the bed and patted the spot beside her. He moved toward her, but when he went to sit down, she held her hand up and palm up. "Spoon first."

With a laugh he handed her the spoon. "Permission to come aboard," he said.

"Permission granted."

He plopped down, kicked his shoes off, and lay beside her. He handed her the ice cream then picked up the book that was in her lap. "What are we reading?" Gavin surveyed the cover and read the back copy. "Sounds pretty good. I mean there's no spaceship or time travel, but you can't have everything." He held the book out to her. "You looked like you were really into it when I showed up. If you want to keep reading, I don't mind."

It was so stupid, but that simple suggestion made her feel like he really understood her. He encouraged her to get lost in fictious worlds, and she appreciated it.

But she'd be a fool to dive into a fantasy world when she had her own fantasy sitting beside her. She placed it on the nightstand. "I have all the entertainment I need right here."

"I hope you don't want me to juggle or dance because I can't do either."

"That's a shame because when you got here, I said to myself, you know what I really could go for? Some juggling."

"Really?"

"Yup, you basically just ruined my night."

"Then I'm just going to have to find a way to make it up to you." He bent his head and captured her lips and leaving her breathless. Her body relaxed and her head spun as his mouth moved against hers.

He pulled back, pressing a chaste kiss to the bridge of her nose. "How'd you break it?" he asked.

"How can you tell?"

He ran his finger down the slope to the top of her nose. "You have a little bump."

It was slight, and while she always found it to be an imperfection, she loved that Gavin noticed it.

"I was reading, head buried in a book not paying attention. My grandma had opened the freezer door, and I walked into it nose first."

"Oh man! That had to have hurt."

"I didn't even care about my nose. I was pissed that I got blood all over my book."

Gavin let out a laugh and fell back on the bed, his hands grabbing at his stomach.

"Go on, laugh it up."

He rolled on his side to face her. He reached up tucking her hair behind her ear. "That is such a Lauren reaction."

She smiled. "Yup. My grandma felt so bad, so while my grandfather sat with me in the emergency room, she went and bought me a new book. I finished the book before we even left the hospital."

"I wouldn't expect anything less."

"What book was it? Do you remember?"

"Of course. It's still one of my favorites to this day. *Outlander*."

"Great series."

"Like you've read it."

"That Jamie Fraser is pretty badass."

"I can't believe you've read *Outlander*."

"It was number two on PBS's The Great American Read. I had to check it out."

"You watched that?"

He nodded, and that was the sexiest thing a man could ever admit.

"I printed out the checklist," she admitted. "I almost have them all checked off."

"What are you missing?"

She counted them off on her hand. "Lord of the Rings, The Chronicles of Narnia, Game of Thrones."

Before she could finish, he grabbed his chest. "You wound me." He fell back dramatically, and she whacked him with a pillow. A laugh bubbled out of her when she pulled the pillow back and saw the amused shock on his face.

"I'm starting to think you're not the bookworm I believed you to be," he said.

"I read hundred-and-fifty books a year. I have earned the badge."

"There's a badge? How come I'm not included in the cool kids club?"

She turned to her nightstand and opened the drawer where she had a bunch of cutout clovers she'd been working on. She turned back to Gavin and grabbed her scissors, cutting the clover into a circle.

"What are you doing over there?" He tried to look, but with a quick twist of her shoulders she blocked his view.

"Don't look," she said.

She grabbed a marker from the drawer and wrote across the paper. With a proud smile, she turned and presented him with the green circle.

He took it from her and laughed as he read, "Cool kids club".

"Consider yourself an honorary member now."

He rubbed at his chin then met her eyes. "You know I'm going to take this with me everywhere now."

"You should. It's a highly coveted club. You should feel special."

"I do," he said and slipped the paper into his pocket.

"You're really going to keep it?"

"Yes," he said matter-of-factly. "I earned it. Though, I think your badge should be revoked for not reading Lord of the Rings. It's blasphemy really."

"I have it on my Kindle. I just haven't gotten to it."

He reached over her, grabbing the e-reader. "This Kindle?"

She nodded.

He turned the device on and searched her library. "Come here," he said, lifting his arm, and she nuzzled into his side. "Get ready to be amazed."

They spent the rest of the night cuddled together while Gavin read to her.

fifteen

Gavin listened to a customer bitch about his day, but he was having a hard time concentrating. His mind kept drifting to last night in Lauren's bed. Nothing happened, but holding her, talking about life, and laughing while she ate her toothpaste ice cream was better than sex.

Getting to know her had been more intimate than any tumble in the sack he'd had. Hearing her laugh was pure ecstasy that filled him with joy and made him want to continue to find ways to make her laugh forever.

The bell above the door chimed, and Gavin took a deep breath as Ashton breezed in like a man on a mission. He took a seat at the bar then stood up, looked down at the stool and moved to the next. It was like watching Goldilocks testing out the three bears porridge until she found the one that was just right. Gavin waited while Ashton searched for a stool that met his approval. Two other customers sat at the far side of the bar having a private conversation. They were just about done with their drinks, and Gavin wouldn't be surprised if they didn't stay for another the way they were hanging all over each other.

"What do I owe the pleasure?" Gavin asked when Ashton finally settled on a stool.

"Can't just come in to say hi to my brother."

Gavin cocked an eyebrow. "Did someone die?"

"No."

"Then no."

"Don't be an ass," Ashton said. "I'll take a scotch when you get a minute."

Gavin reached for the bottle and poured Ashton a double, then pushed the glass across the bar to him. Ashton held the glass up and took a sip.

The couple waved Gavin over, and he closed out their tab, handing them their card back and being grateful that they left a ten on the bar before heading out. When the door closed, Ashton nodded toward the mess in the corner.

"How's the construction going?" He glanced over to the unfinished mess. "It doesn't look like much has been done?" Ashton asked.

Gavin bit his tongue, debating if he should tell his brother. He pushed his pride aside. "I'm out of money."

"What do you mean you're out of money? I gave you plenty."

"I know that, and it's not like I went to Vegas for a week and blew it on slot machines and hookers for crying out loud. It went toward the cost of the building."

"I don't understand what the issue is then."

Gavin suppressed his anger. Ashton's last loan was the reason Gavin was even able to keep the bar. He needed to look beyond the fact that Ashton was his brother and realize he was an investor. He couldn't let his emotions get the best of him especially because he would never do that if it were anyone else. He took a deep breath.

"I started doing some renovations. I thought they

would be minor but…"

Ashton glanced at him with understanding. "It turned into a nightmare?"

Taken aback by the lack of animosity, Gavin stared at Ashton for a moment before explaining. "Pretty much and now the cost quadrupled, and if I can't get the money together to get this fixed then, there's going to be a corner permanently under yellow tape."

"How much do you need?" Ashton asked matter-of-factly.

"Another ten grand."

Ashton reached into his coat pocket and pulled out his checkbook. He took a pen from his other pocket, clicked it, and scribbled across the check. With a quick rip, he handed the check to Gavin.

"That's it?" Gavin asked. It was almost too easy. "You don't want to lecture me about handling my money better or using my head before I start knocking down walls?" He was prepared for the lecture, expected it really.

"Shit happens," Ashton said. "And sometimes it's out of your control."

Gavin's eyes closed as realization set in. "Lily May told you, didn't she?"

"Not exactly."

Gavin's eyebrow arched in curiosity.

"She may have told me that you would be coming to me for something and then told me to think about my own recent problems before jumping the gun."

"That's why you're here then. She told you this, what?

Yesterday?"

"Thirty minutes before I got here. I'm sure she'll be calling in ten to make sure I didn't string you up somewhere."

Gavin laughed. "I'd like to see you try."

"Is that a challenge?"

"Nah." Ashton tugged at the bottom of his sleeves. "Wouldn't want to ruin my suit."

"Likely story." Gavin smirked. "Want another scotch?"

"I'm going to head back home and spend time with my girl. Between the expansion and the gala, I feel like we've barely had a minute without talking about work."

"My have times changed." Ashton used to live, breath, and eat work, and nobody could get him to take a break. Lily May wasn't only a sweet girl, she was exactly what his brother needed. Even though their own relationship hadn't always been rainbows and sunshine, he was happy to have Ashton back in his life. "I can still count on you to be at the gala, right?"

Oh, that gala. The one time a year Gavin had to don a monkey suit and rub elbows with all the elite assholes Ashton dealt with on a daily basis. It was as fun as what he imagined getting a back wax would be. But it was an event Ashton started because of their dad's struggle with diabetes. The gala was less about Ashton and Seattle's elite and more about spotlighting a cause that affects hundreds of thousands of people and had affected their own family. Raising money for research, providing medical care for the less fortunate and for children was the real reason Gavin bit his tongue and made an appearance. He might not have liked the life Ashton lived with the high-power career and endless streams of money, but Gavin appreciated what his brother did with it. He wasn't just a jackass who stuffed his own pockets. He gave back, and the least Gavin could do was show up.

"I'll be there."

"Good. Have you gone by to see Dad and Pops?"

"I haven't had time. Besides, I'll see them at the gala."

"That's a week away."

"So?" Gavin doubted much would happen between then and now. He could catch up with them then when other people were around to distract them from asking him too many questions about his life.

"All I'm saying is it wouldn't hurt to drop by to see them."

Gavin held up the check. "Thanks for the money. You can add it to my loan."

"Don't worry about it."

"I'm paying you back whether you want me to or not."

"Just get it taken care of."

"I plan on it. I don't want anyone else getting hurt."

"What do you mean anyone else?" Ashton's voice deepened to his boardroom tone.

"A friend of mine, Lauren, you might have met her. She tripped and hurt her foot."

"How bad?"

"It's just a sprain. She went to the doctor."

"She went to the doctor? How am I just hearing about

this now?"

Gavin looked at Ashton like he was insane. "It wasn't that big of a deal. I took her, and she'll be fine."

"Not that big of a deal? You do realize who I am, right?"

"How can I forget? You seem to remind me every single chance you get."

"Then you know how people go out of their way to sue me for any little thing just so they can get their hands on a slither of my fortune."

"Lauren isn't going to sue you."

"How do you know that? How well do you actually know this girl?"

Gavin's anger rose, his fingers clenched, his nails dug into the calluses skin of his hands. "She's friends with Lily May for crying out loud. Besides, I know her well enough, and as far as I'm concerned this conversation is over."

Ashton held his hands up in front of him as if that would be the needed peace treaty to make Gavin's heightened anger simmer down. Ashton was out of his damn mind if he thought that would work. He came into Gavin's bar and was now talking about his girl!

His girl… that was something he'd have to think about later, but right now he needed to deal with his jack off of a brother.

"Look," Ashton said. "I have had people I thought I could trust come after me for less. Money makes people do stupid shit. I want to believe that this girl isn't one of them, but I've been screwed one too many times to not be suspicious."

"That sucks, but Lauren isn't like that."

"How do you know?"

Gavin's blood boiled over. "Because I do!" he yelled, his voice echoing through the bar, his veins feeling like they were going to break free of his neck and ricochet off the damn walls. "I just do."

Ashton held his hands up again, and the skin along Gavin's jaw tightened.

"I'm sorry I just need to cover all my bases here. This would be a media frenzy, and I can't take any chances right now especially with my international deal about to be finalized."

"You have my word your precious business will be fine," Gavin said through clenched teeth.

"Don't get pissy with me."

Gavin crossed his arms over his chest and leaned against the bar. He hadn't even begun to get pissy. If Ashton accused Lauren of malicious intent one more time, he would show Ashton what it was to be pissy.

"I'm going to take your word for it, but if you think for even a second that she might have an ulterior motive, call me."

"I can promise you I won't be calling."

"I sincerely hope so."

Gavin didn't believe that for a second. Ashton loved when Gavin found himself in a bind and needed Ashton to dig him out. "I'm sure you do. You would love for this to backfire on me so you can play the damn hero."

Ashton picked up his coat and slid it on. "I hate that you think of me that way."

Gavin scoffed. "I have reason to." Ever since Gavin turned down Ashton's offer to work with him, he felt like Ashton secretly hoped Gavin would fail.

"I thought we were over this bullshit."

"I thought we were too." Gavin might have felt that Ashton was rooting for him to fail, but deep down Gavin knew it wasn't true.

Ashton caught his eye. "So what you're just going to hate me again?"

Gavin let out a breath and shook his head. He didn't want to hate Ashton, he didn't even want to be mad at him, but sometimes Ashton was really impossible to understand. Still he tried to put himself in Ashton's shoes. He was a self-made billionaire who fought through hell to get to where he was today, and so many people tried to take that away from him. He'd spent countless dollars killing stories and settling with liars out of court just to make them go away. It only made sense that he would be suspicious of everyone. If Gavin wasn't mistaken, he was pretty sure Ashton was suspicious of Lily May when they first met. It's just who he was, and Gavin could accept that even if the accusation pissed him off.

"No," he said. "I don't hate you again. I've never hated you."

"Just wanted to piss in my Cheerios."

"Something like that."

"Does that mean we're good then?" Ashton asked.

"We're good. Get the hell out of here and back to your girlfriend."

Ashton held his hand out to Gavin, and he accepted the friendly peace offer. "Get that fixed," he said, motioning to the area as he headed to the door. "And if you need money stop being a stubborn asshole and just call."

Before Gavin could throw a sarcastic retort in his direction, the door closed and the bar was silent.

A sappy look spread across Ginny's face. "That's irrelevant. Now go sit down."

"I got it, it's no big deal." Just because Lauren had a little ankle injury, didn't mean she wasn't capable of making a little dip.

Ginny sighed, resting her back against the counter. "You're hurt and should be resting. I'm making the dip."

"But I can do it."

Ginny shook her head. "I don't doubt that, but let me handle this."

Lauren jutted out her bottom lip. "Please don't ask me to go sit. I may lose my mind."

Ginny pointed to the corner by the sink with a smirk. "Fine, you can stay, but stand over there so you're not in the way."

Ashlynn walked into the kitchen and dropped her bag on the counter. Without a word she went in the fridge and grabbed the wine. She didn't even bother with a glass, popping the cork and drinking right out of the bottle.

"Rough day?" Lauren asked.

"Rough would be putting it lightly." She took another swig from the bottle.

Lauren laughed. "Good thing we have more wine. You're about to drink us out of house and home."

Ashlynn took another swig, then put the bottle down, swiping a hand across her lips. "Nope, I'm good now."

"You okay?" Ginny asked.

"Fine." Ashlynn tossed her hair over her shoulder. "But don't be surprised if I wind up on the five o'clock news for murdering my coworker."

Lauren winced. "That bad, huh?"

"I want to physically hurt him." Ashlynn rolled her eyes. "He's just so smug like he's God's gift to the world. If anything, he's God's way of punishing me for every wrong doing I've done in life."

"Just ignore him," Ginny said.

"I wish I could, but today my boss put me on a project with him, so I'm stuck dealing with him for the foreseeable future."

"Sorry," Ash." Lauren had lucked out. She loved everyone she worked with.

"No biggie. I'm a big girl. I'll deal with it. Now that I'm feeling good, what do you need me to do?"

"We're just getting chips together," Lauren explained.

Ashlynn waved her hand toward the living room. "Go sit down, and I'll take care of it."

Lauren's jaw tensed, teeth clenched.

"Dangerous words," Ginny warned. "Watch out or she might hurt you."

Ashlynn held her hands up. "I come in peace."

"Sorry, I've been holed up in my bed all day."

"You love to stay in your bed though." Ashlynn glanced at her. "It's the first place you go when you get home and you would stay there all night if we let you."

"I know! I have no idea what's wrong with me."

"I do," Ginny said.

Lauren cocked an eyebrow in her direction, and Ginny smiled but didn't say anything.

"I bet if I was home in bed on my own things would be different, but because I'm being forced to be here it's different."

Ashlynn shrugged. "If you say so."

"We're here," Jemma called from the front door. She came into the kitchen with Olivia trailing behind.

Olivia rested her hand on her stomach. "I just have to change out of these dress pants before this button pops, and I take out an eye."

"Please do," Jemma said. "I like both of my eyes exactly how they are, thank you very much."

Olivia disappeared to her room, and Lily May showed up with and overfilled charcuterie board. Lauren didn't even know how she managed to carry it into the house without the help of a crane. She clicked over to the coffee table in her sky-high heels and placed it down. "Dig in!"

Everyone dove right in, gathering a collection of meats, cheeses, and crackers on their plates before taking their usual spots around the living room.

Lauren ate a piece of prosciutto wrapped around some kind of cheese that was the equivalent of cheesy goodness and immediately went for another.

"I think Olivia might have got taken out by her own pants." Jemma laughed. "Maybe someone should go check on her."

"She's probably checking her notifications. Liv!" Ashlynn called out, her voice echoing through the living room.

"While we wait," Lily May adjusted her top. "Lauren,

what are you wearing to the gala?"

Lauren looked at her, eyebrows pulling together. "I'm not going to the gala."

"Gavin hasn't asked you?" Lily May asked.

"No," Lauren admitted. "But I thought he was going with Rae?"

"He was, but I invited Tommy, so technically he no longer has a date."

Lauren shrugged, trying not to let the disappointment that was tugging at her gut show. "Maybe he wants to fly solo."

Lily May appeared unconvinced. "The whole reason he signed up for that dating app was to find a date."

"And he did. He found Rae," Lauren said.

Olivia walked into the living room and grabbed a plate. "I thought Rae was dating Tommy."

Jemma rolled her eyes. "She is, but before they started dating, Gavin and Rae matched up on a dating site, and Gavin asked her to the gala. Lily May has since invited Tommy. Sheesh keep up."

"I'm trying, but this is more complicated than an episode of Jerry Springer."

"Please don't compare my life to Jerry Springer," Lauren said.

"Just calling it as I see it," Olivia said.

"What Olivia is trying to say," Ashlynn interrupted. "Is that it seems complicated, but if Rae and Tommy are both going to the gala then that means Rae won't be going with Gavin, which means Gavin needs a date, so why hasn't he asked you?"

Lauren shrugged. "I have no idea."

"He's been here like every day since you hurt yourself," Olivia said, plopping down on the couch and taking a bite of a cracker.

He had been. Every morning before the bar opened, he would stop by with breakfast and that adorable smile. He'd ask her about her ankle, then look at it himself because he never took her word that she was okay. He needed to see it for himself. He would get her an ice pack if she needed it or help her get a mug down for her tea. It was the best way to start her day, and she was sad when she would have to go back to work. She was getting used to their routine.

She thought what they had was special, but maybe it wasn't all that special. Not special enough to invite her to the gala at least. Who knew, maybe him coming over had nothing to do with the fact that he liked her, and more to do with feeling guilty that she got hurt in his bar and he felt marginally responsible.

She'd read one too many books and she was letting her imagination get away with her. Gavin wasn't the type to deceive her like that. He had a lot on his mind, especially now with the St. Patrick's Day event at the bar; he probably wasn't even thinking about the gala.

There was no reason for Lauren to think about it either. Besides, that's not what tonight was about.

"Can we talk about the book now?"

"The guy was a moron," Jemma said, and Lauren smiled, sinking into the couch.

seventeen

Gavin pulled up to his childhood home and killed the engine. He loved his dads more than anything on the planet, but coming home, seeing them, he had always felt like a failure who lived in the shadows of Ashton, the golden boy whose success went beyond anything Gavin could ever dream of.

He hated feeling that way, but he had no control over it. Even if he forced the thoughts to the back of his mind, they still managed to pop up at the most random time, reminding him that he would never be the one who their dads were proudest of.

Ashton was right though. Gavin hadn't been by to see them in a while, and it wasn't fair to them that he couldn't get over his own insecurities because despite his feelings of failure, Dad and Pops never once ever made him feel inferior to Ashton.

He got to the front door and rang the bell. He could have walked in, but since he hadn't been by for some time, he almost felt as if he no longer deserved to just stroll into their lives unannounced.

The door flung open, and Pops' eyes widened. "What are you doing here?" he asked, throwing his arms around Gavin with so much gusto he practically knocked Gavin back out onto the street.

"Been a while," Gavin said. "Thought I'd stop by. Hope it's a good time."

"Stop that! It's always a good time. And you don't have to ring the bell."

"I didn't know if I'd be interrupting something."

"You are always more important than whatever we're doing. Now come in. Are you hungry? I can whip something up for you."

"I ate before I left."

"I'll get a few bags of chips then. Nothing big, just something to snack on." Gavin didn't bother to argue. Pops loved to feed people, and the more you told him you weren't hungry, the more he would try to make you eat something.

"Chips would be great," Gavin said.

"Follow me to the kitchen then."

Gavin did, looking around the house and trying to figure out where Dad was. He expected him to hurry in from wherever he was to greet him, but there was no sign of him.

"Where's Dad?"

"On the phone with Lily May, going over a few things for the gala."

Gavin forced a smile and darted to the fridge before Pops could start questioning him about his date and what he's planning on wearing. He grabbed a bottle of sparkling water and shut the fridge ready to change the subject, but he didn't have to. Pops clearly took the hint.

Pops opened a bag of chips and dumped the contents into a large china bowl. "How's being a business owner going?"

"Great." He took the bowl and led the way into the living room. Gavin placed the bowl on the coffee table, and he and Pops both sat down on the sofa. Gavin immediately reached for the chips. Since they were there he might as well eat them. "I'm going to be doing a St. Patrick's Day event. You and Dad should stop by and check the place out."

Pops rested his hand on his chest, an honored look in his eyes. "We will. Do you need help with anything?"

"Lauren has helped me with most of it. I think we're good."

Pops eyebrow lifted and Gavin just kept talking before Pops played a game of twenty questions. "They'll be karaoke and if you can give me a recipe for Irish soda bread that'd be great."

"I can definitely do that."

Pops looked at him, and Gavin slowly chewed until he swallowed, but Pops still stared at him in the way that made Gavin feel like he needed to confess all his sins. "What?" he finally said.

"Are you happy?" Pops asked.

Gavin thought about Devin and how miserable he always was, bitching about a job he hated and a boss he despised. Then he thought about how lucky he felt that he was able to give the guy some reprieve even if it was for only a few hours a few times a week. Gavin didn't need to go anywhere to escape his life, and now that he took a moment to think about it and bring things into perspective, he could answer Pops with the truth.

"I am." It was more than just his job too. With Lauren

in his life he felt lighter, and looked forward to seeing her. That anticipation kept him smiling all day and night.

"That's all Dad and I care about."

"I just assumed because I don't wear a suit every day and throw you a gala every year…"

Pops sighed. "It's been twenty-six years. When are you going to stop comparing yourself to your brother?"

"It's kind of hard not to."

"You and Ashton are two totally different people. What makes him happy is not what makes you happy. Are we proud of him and everything he's accomplished? Absolutely."

He was the richest man in Seattle, and his business was expanding every day, now going global and creating the empire he always dreamed about. He was the definition of success, and Gavin was… a bar owner.

"But Dad and I are proud of you too," Pops said.

Gavin rolled his eyes. "You don't have to give me the pity speech. It's fine."

"Who said anything about pity?"

He shrugged, but in mid-shrug, Pops grabbed his shoulders and urged Gavin to look him in the eye.

"We don't pity you. It's absurd you'd even think that. We are proud of you. We don't care about how much you have in the bank or how many buildings you own. All that is meaningless. What's important is that you have always stayed true to who you are. Ashton gave you many opportunities to go against the grain and join his ranks and you refused. You stood your ground, adamant about making your own path in the world. And with your bar, you have. It might not be as big a carbon footprint as Ashton, but even the smallest marks in the world can make a big impact."

Gavin might not have enough money in the bank to buy a small country, but Pops was right. He was still making his mark in the world. And maybe it was small in the grand scheme of things, but when you narrowed it down, it wasn't small at all. Not to the patrons of his bar, the ones who relied on him for a cold drink, a good time, and sometimes just a friend. He gave them that and at the end of the day, he made a difference for them. Hell, it made a difference for him.

Ashton loved money and Gavin loved people. They might have been born only a minute apart, but despite looking similar they were total opposites, and comparing himself to his brother was something he needed to stop doing. Gavin didn't want to resent Ashton. Not anymore at least. Ashton was a major pain in his ass, but he loved his brother with every ounce of his heart. Not that he'd ever tell him that.

"You're right," Gavin finally said to Pops. "I can still leave my stamp on the world just in my own way."

"You've already started." Pops shucked his chin. "I finally found out why you didn't make it home for Christmas."

Not this again. Gavin refrained from rolling his eyes. "I told you I was working."

"Yes, you did, but what you forgot to mention is that you opened the bar so people who didn't have anywhere to go for Christmas had somewhere to have a free meal."

"How'd you find out?" Gavin asked. It had been right before he'd bought the bar and basically destroyed it with construction. Some of the regulars had stopped by with homemade dishes they volunteered to make. It was a small event, but it was still more than what those people would have had and he was happy that he was able to give that to them.

"I have my ways. I just don't understand why you didn't tell us. I would have stopped laying on the guilt trip."

Gavin laughed. "No, you wouldn't have."

"Okay fine, maybe I wouldn't have, but I would have at least taken it down a few notches."

Gavin didn't mean to keep it a secret, but he didn't see what he did as some big charity event like Ashton's gala. He just opened his doors for people who didn't have somewhere to be. He felt bad for missing Christmas with his dads, but he knew no matter what they'd be surrounded by plenty of people who loved them. The people who came into his bar that day didn't have anyone. It was the least Gavin could do.

"You and Dad always taught us about kindness, about passing on goodwill and knowing how lucky we are. One of my regulars told me he had no where to go for Christmas, and I decided to open. I cooked a few things, some people brought trays of food, and I had free pitchers of beer and wine. Honestly, it was nothing."

"To those people, it was everything." Pops hugged him and kissed the top of his head just like he did when Gavin was a kid. "When Dad and I used to take you and Ashton to the soup kitchens, we hoped that you would carry those experiences with you, and it fills my heart to see you being proactive in giving back and making other people happy."

"It felt good," he admitted. "I think I want to make it an annual thing."

"If that's the case then, Dad and I will be there with bells on."

"Really?" On Christmas their door was always open and people would stop in and out all day, bringing food and presents. The fact that Pops was willing to leave that behind to come hang out in a hole in the wall for him warmed his heart.

"Of course!" Pops said. "I'll even make a few dishes and get Lily May to drag your workaholic brother."

Gavin laughed, imagining Ashton spending his Christmas in a bar. "I bet he'll love that."

"If Lily May is there, I'm sure he won't even care. Who knows. It'll be what seven months from now; maybe they'll be a Christmas proposal we can celebrate."

"You're really getting ahead of yourself," Gavin said.

"I know, but they are just so perfect for each other. She really softens his hard edges."

Ever since Lily May came into Ashton's life, he'd been much more tolerable. They were perfect for each other.

"And I didn't want to bring it up, but since we're on the subject…You plan on bringing someone to the gala?"

"As a matter of fact, I am." He hadn't asked her yet, but he was planning on it and he knew she didn't have class that night. He'd finally get to take her out on a real date. It couldn't get much fancier than the gala either. An invitation was sought after by some of the richest people in the country and Lauren deserved to be there and experience it.

He remembered his first gala and it was definitely a sight to see. Nothing his brain could properly imagine and with Lily May taking charge this year and planning the event, Gavin had a feeling it would be over the top and amazing. Thinking about Lauren with a smile on her face, looking around the place in awe as they made their way through the event made him unbelievably happy.

Just being with her made him unbelievably happy. Talking to her, thinking about her, he couldn't control the flood of joy that filled him from those simple acts.

Pops gasped, slapping a hand over his mouth. "Tell me all about her. Is it serious? It's serious, isn't it?"

"It's a date. Don't go planning our wedding or anything crazy like that." Though, marrying Lauren, as crazy as it sounded, also sounded exactly right. "And please don't scare her off with a million questions. I really like this girl. She's kind of amazing and she makes me happy."

Pops' eyes shown bright as he stared at Gavin, his hand resting against his lips.

"Why are you looking at me like that?" Gavin asked.

"Because I see it now."

"See what?"

"You aren't just happy. You're in love."

"What are you talking about?"

"I didn't notice it before, but now I see it, you're

different. Your shoulders aren't so tense, your eyes are a little less squinty like you're waiting for the inevitable doom."

"First of all, I never looked like that."

"Mmm hmm," Dad said, coming into the living room and giving Gavin a big hug.

Gavin pulled back. "I did not."

Dad laughed. "You keep thinking that."

Gavin moved to the loveseat, and Dad sat down on the couch next to Pops, resting his hand on Pop's knee. They looked at each other; and Gavin knew that look all too well. They were silently agreeing with each other while simultaneously having a secret conversation.

"What?" Gavin said when their eyebrows kept moving, but their lips didn't.

"We can't wait to meet her," Dad said.

"Please don't scare her off."

Pops swatted his hand. "We would never."

Gavin arched an eyebrow. "May I remind you of the last girl I brought home for you to meet?"

"She wasn't good for you," Pops said.

"Why, because she didn't like your goulash?"

"Everybody likes my goulash."

Gavin laughed, and Dad nodded. "You can't argue there," Dad said.

"That's not a reason not to like someone though."

"She wasn't the one," Pops said. "Dad and I know you better than anyone, and trust us, that girl didn't deserve you."

Cynthia was a little on the needy side and not to

mention materialistic. She was a good kisser, but there was no spark whatsoever, and no matter how good someone kissed, if there wasn't that little zing of unexplained excitement, it wasn't worth a thing.

Lauren on the other hand, it wasn't just a spark; it was a whole damn firework display. He never experienced anything like that in his life. Every time their lips touched it was like his entire being went up in a glory of smoke and flames. His body became an electrical conductor, dispersing the current through every inch of him.

"I hope you like Lauren," he said, trying to keep the stupid grin off his face. "Because I really hope she's going to be around for a long time."

"Oh my god," Dad said, squeezing Pops' hand. "You were right. Our boy has gone and got shot by Cupid's arrow."

"Oh geez that's my cue to leave." Gavin stood.

Pops jumped up from the couch. "Wait!" He held his hand out like he was stopping traffic. "You haven't told us anything about this Lauren. Pretty name by the way."

Gavin smiled. "You're just going to have to wait until you meet her."

"Don't you dare walk out of this house, young man," Dad said as Gavin made his way to the front door. He could feel both his dads hot on his heels, and he knew no matter how much he wanted to leave without giving them a single answer, he would never be able to. They would hop into his car or hold onto the bumper, refusing to let go until he threw them a bone to chew on.

"I'm glad I stopped by," he said, turning toward them. "I'll see you at the gala." He hugged each of them, ignoring the stubborn arch of their eyebrows.

He opened the door and turned back to them. "She's a librarian who has a smile that smacks you in the face. Her laugh is like the first notes of a great song. Slow to build, but once it reaches its crescendo, you're hooked. She's kind, always has a book in her bag, and she makes me happy."

Dad squealed, and Pops clapped.

"And that's all I'm telling you. Bye, love you guys." Gavin hurried out the door before either one could start a game of twenty questions.

eighteen

It had only been a few days, but the swelling had finally gone down on Lauren's ankle, and she was finally able to put pressure on it without seeing stars. It still hurt, but the pain was tolerable as long as she took it easy. She got dressed early and made a cup of lemon ginger tea before settling on the couch.

Everyone had left for the day, and she was sick of sitting in her bedroom. She took a sip and picked up her Kindle. She was eager to know what happened next in the *The Fellowship of the Ring,* but she'd promised Gavin she wouldn't read ahead without him.

He had already texted her to let her know he wouldn't be by this morning. He finally had a contractor coming to the bar to take care of the mess so he could get his customer base back.

St. Patrick's Day was the best way to kickstart this new chapter for the Hole in the Wall. She grabbed her laptop. He needed to get word out, and the best way to do that was good old social media. She created a graphic and posted it on her page asking her friends to share.

Within an hour she had twenty shares and a bunch of comments from people who said they would definitely stop by and check it out. She took a picture of the screen and texted it to Gavin with the message: *The event of the year is a go!*

She had no doubt that St. Patrick's Day at the bar was

going to be a success, but the event of the year was definitely the gala, and Gavin still hadn't asked her. She tried not to think about it much, but being home all day with not much to do, it was hard not to.

Did he not think she was gala material? She didn't own a dress that would be worthy of such an occasion, but she could rent one and have Jemma do her hair. She could clean up nicely if given the chance. Not that she felt like her every day attire was all that bad.

"Okay enough," she said to herself. "You're being ridiculous."

She got up from the couch, putting a little too much pressure on her bum ankle. Pain shot through her leg right up her calf and into her thigh. She jumped to the other foot and felt instant relief, but the pain still radiated at the center of her ankle.

"Just as well." She looked down at her ankle. "I probably wouldn't even be able to wear nice shoes."

This was stupid. She grabbed her keys, got in the car, and headed toward the Hole in the Wall. The entire drive to the bar she tried to convince herself to turn around, but that was the old Lauren and she was done hiding from life.

She had a question that needed an answer to, and the only way to get it was to go to the source itself. Twenty minutes later she found a spot on the street by the bar and put her car in park. She got out, adjusting her skirt, and headed to the front door.

She didn't exactly have a plan, but she wasn't expecting to walk in to a full on construction site. Sheets of plastic hung around the bar, protecting the taps and bottles from the dust. Two men worked on the wires while three others were picking up broken pieces of wall and floor.

Gavin was talking to one of the men, and she realized that her timing was terrible. She knew he was busy this morning. She backed up toward the door, but Gavin spotted her. His eyebrows knitted together, but his lips quirked at the edges.

"What are you doing here?" he asked, and all the men turned and looked at her.

"I um…" She wasn't about to tell him why she was here while they had an audience. She shifted from one foot to the other forgetting about her ankle and putting a little too much pressure on it. She winced as the pain radiated up her calf.

Gavin was at her side in a blink of an eye, wrapping his arm around her waist and anchoring her to him. "You should be resting," he said.

She was so sick of resting. "I'm fine."

"You don't look fine."

Before she lost her courage, she took a deep breath and met his gaze. "Why don't you want me to go to the gala with you?"

His eyes widened, and it felt like he stumbled back a bit. She was a bit shocked at herself, but she just wanted to know why. They had still yet to go on a date though it could easily be because of the whole jacking up her ankle, but what if it was because he didn't want to be seen with her in public?

Okay, that was ridiculous and she knew it, but damn it

this was driving her insane. She couldn't think of any other reason except she wasn't fancy like Lily May with her perfectly tailored clothes. Lauren's skirts were always wrinkled from cuddling up with a book. "Are you embarrassed by me?"

"What? No! Of course not."

She might as well have slapped him the way his face contorted. She stepped out of his hold, realizing how out of her mind she was being. Red hot waves of embarrassment spread through her, filling her chest and cheeks.

"Let's pretend this never happened," she said and turned to the door, but Gavin grabbed her hand and swung her back to him.

"You are not running away now," he said.

She stared at her feet; she was such an idiot. He rested his finger gently under her chin and urged her to look at him. She met his deep green eyes and let out a sigh. "I'm sorry. I shouldn't have come. It was just Lily May asked me what I was wearing to the gala the other night, and I told her I wasn't invited, and she seemed surprised, which made me wonder…I don't know. I should've let it go."

"Will you go to the gala with me?" he asked.

"I don't want a pity invite," she said. She'd rather never go on a date again than be a pity date.

"It's not a pity invite."

"Yes, it is."

He shook his head. "I was planning on asking you, but I was a little scared."

"Scared? Of what? You were going to go with Rae, so

what's the difference?"

"When I had invited Rae, it was because I didn't want to show up to the gala single because with Ashton no longer single, my dads would be on my case about meeting someone. I liked Rae, but with you and me, it's different. I was afraid of my dads asking you too many questions and scaring you off."

"I don't scare too easily."

"My dads will probably ask you what colors you have in mind for our wedding."

Lauren laughed. "I think I can handle that."

"Then is that a yes?"

She nodded. "That's a yes."

"Thank God." He bent down and scooped her off her feet, and she let out a startled laugh.

"What are you doing?"

"Getting you off of that foot. I'm done here and am just in the guys' way. How about we go upstairs and read a little Fellowship of the Rings."

"Keep talking dirty to me," she said.

"We can make some herbal tea."

"Mmm. What kind?"

"I bought lemon ginger the other day."

Her head fell back, and she moaned. "That's so hot."

"I'll even let you wear one of my hoodies."

She grabbed her chest and dramatically let her head flop back. "Okay, stop, it's too much for me to handle."

He laughed, and she hooked her arms around his neck, holding tight and grateful she took the risk.

nineteen

It was the night of the gala, and Lauren abandoned her tights and flared skirts for a form fitted gold shimmery number that molded to her body like a glove. It wasn't something she'd ever choose for herself, but Lily May refused to leave the store unless Lauren agreed to buy it. When Lauren tried to use the price tag as an excuse to get out of it, Lily May scooped it up and brought it over to the register herself, handing over her American Express without as much as a flutter of her long eyelashes.

She felt beautiful as she looked at her reflection in the floor length mirror. Jemma had done her hair, and Olivia did her makeup. She had no idea how much a little blush could brighten up her entire face.

She heard the knock on the door, and butterflies swarmed in her stomach. She couldn't wait for Gavin to see her. She hoped he liked what he saw since it was so drastic from what she usually wore. There was only one way to find out. With one final glance in the mirror, she turned on the strappy gold heels that so far weren't killing her.

The swelling in her ankle was completely gone, but the black and blue still lingered. She put a little concealer on it and covered it the best she could. She doubted most people would look down at her ankle long enough to even notice.

She heard Gavin and Olivia talking as she stepped out

of her room and into the living room. Gavin looked refined and gorgeous in a fashionable navy-blue tuxedo with a black lapel and black bow tie.

The conversation ceased when Gavin's eyes landed on her. His lips parted, and his eyes grew large. She shifted uncomfortably, not sure if he was liking what he was seeing.

"You look. My god. Wow. You're stunning."

Her cheeks heated at the compliment and the genuine tone in his voice. "Thank you. I had some help."

"Wow," he said.

"You too. I love the blue."

His eyes scanned her up and down again. "Wow."

"You said that already."

"It's all I can manage right now."

"Our girl is smokin'," Olivia exclaimed. "You better show her the time of her life."

"I plan on it," Gavin said.

"Have fun you two," Olivia gave a wave as she headed to her bedroom, leaving her and Gavin alone.

Gavin took her hand, and pressed his lips to her knuckles. "I'd kiss you properly, but I don't want to mess up your lipstick."

Lauren laughed. "The one downfall to getting pretty. It can be messy."

"You're always pretty."

She went to slide her teeth over her bottom lip, then thought better of it. The last thing she needed was lipstick on her teeth. "Thanks," she said instead.

"You ready?" He held his arm out to her, and she

looped hers through his.

"Let's do this."

They got in Gavin's car and headed to the event. It was a twenty-minute drive, and the entire time Lauren was very aware of Gavin. The car smelled like him, a delicious combination of citrus and pine. It was crisp and refreshing.

His hand found hers, and he laced his fingers through hers. She loved how effortlessly he did things. Like he didn't think; he just did, and it was as natural as being.

"What are you thinking?" Gavin asked.

"What the gala is going to be like. I have never been to one before."

"I've been to many but never one Lily May planned. I can imagine it'll be over the top and memorable."

Lauren smiled. "Just like her. I can't wait."

"She told me she'd help us with the St. Patrick's Day Extravaganza."

Us. The single world sent a rush of giddiness through her.

"I hope that's okay."

"Why wouldn't it be? Lily May does event planning for a living. We'd be crazy not to tap into that head of hers."

"I just hope I don't wind up with sheep in my bar because I wouldn't put it past her."

Lauren laughed, imagining a sheep in the bar and Lily May unable to understand why it wasn't a good idea. "I think you need to get sheep now."

"Definitely not."

"You're no fun."

"Oh, but I am."

She couldn't argue there.

They pulled onto the street of the venue and waited in line for the valet. It was a quick process that ran efficiently, and Lauren wouldn't expect anything less from an event planned by Lily May.

Gavin took her arm as flashes from the paparazzi blinded them and guided her toward the man dressed like a ring master taking the coveted tickets.

"Step right up," he said to the people behind them.

"Is that a red carpet?" Lauren asked, looking at the red floor stretched out in front of them. To the right of the carpet, a pocket of cameraman all vied to get Gavin's attention. "This is crazy. They know your name."

"I'm Ashton's twin, so they know me by default."

"Even still it's pretty cool."

"If you say so," Gavin said, running a hand through his hair. "Come on, let's keep moving."

They walked the red carpet, and Lauren felt like a Hollywood starlet. Gavin obliged one photographer who asked for a picture, but then he hurried her into the building.

Servers moved about wearing white shirts with red suspenders and red bow ties. Red and white curtains draped from the ceiling to mimic a circus tent and gold tablecloths with carousel horses rose up out of the tables surrounding a dance floor. Aerial dancers hung from colorful sheets from the ceiling, contorting into unnatural poses yet making it look as natural as walking.

A bearded woman sauntered through the crowd with a

man sporting a handlebar mustache, and a black leotard who held a barbell above his head. A sad clown with a red painted nose and black vertical lines drawn from his eyebrows to his cheek moseyed by them, letting out a pitiful sigh as he went. Old-fashioned signs pointed them in directions to games, popcorn and prizes.

It was breathtakingly beautiful as well as mind blowing in size and detail. Lily May captured the true essence of a vintage carnival, and it was as if Lauren stepped through a time portal when she walked through the door.

Beyond that were carnival games with prizes ranging from stuffed animals to trips to various locations around the world. Of course for your chance to win those, you had to pony up more money than Lauren made in a year. Yet, people crowded the place to take their turn.

Lauren held tight to Gavin as he seemed like he knew how to maneuver the event. He dipped in and out of people, stopping every now and again to talk with celebrities and socialites Lauren recognized from the tabloids.

She leaned into him. "You know a lot of famous people."

"I wouldn't consider it more than that. I see them at Ashton's events, and that's it. It's not like I call them up to grab a beer."

"It's still cool that they know your name. Admit it." She poked his stomach, and he jumped back, but she poked again.

He grimaced. "Okay, it is a little cool."

"Knew it."

"You look so proud of yourself right now."

"I am."

"Gavin!" A man with short salt and pepper hair approached. He was a good-looking older guy with a wide smile and a sparkle in his eye. Beside him was another man who was slightly taller and whose smile was just as warm but not nearly as wide. "You're here." The man threw his arms around Gavin and pulled him tight.

"You must be Lauren," the other gentleman said. "My son has told me a lot about you."

"Oh! You're Gavin's dads."

"You can call me Pops, everyone else does."

"It's a pleasure to meet you." Lauren held her hand out and gave Pops a proper greeting. He had a strong grip, but it was more welcoming than it was intimidating.

"And this is Dad or Bill as everyone else calls him." Gavin patted the other gentleman's chest.

"A pleasure to meet you as well."

"When Gavin told us he had met someone we were so happy," Pops said.

"You raised an amazing man." Heat filled her cheeks when she caught Gavin's gaze.

Bill glowed at the compliment. "He turned out all right."

Pops laughed.

"Have you been to the game section yet?" Bill asked.

Gavin glanced over to the area then shook his head. "We just got here."

"Then you have to go over there. It's really something

else. You know what, I'll bring you myself."

Bill rested his arm over her shoulders. "We have much to talk about." He geared her toward the game section, and Lauren didn't even mind. Dad and Pops were everything Gavin had described and she was excited to get to know them better.

***

An hour later, Lauren officially loved Gavin's dads. She couldn't remember the last time she had so much fun. While his dads were talking to some guy in a fancy tuxedo, Gavin leaned his mouth against her ear. "Dance with me."

"I thought you said you couldn't dance or juggle."

"I can't, but it's an excuse to hold you, and I'm taking it."

"How can a girl say no to that?"

"Simple, you can't." He took her hand and guided her to the dance floor. His hands snaked around her waist as they swayed to the music. At one point, Lauren wasn't even sure what music was playing; all she could concentrate on was Gavin.

"This place is out of control!" Tommy's voice penetrated her Gavin bubble, and she lifted her head off of Gavin's chest to see Rae and Tommy coming to a stop in front of them.

Rae looked beautiful in a purple dress that made her red hair pop. Tommy was in a t-shirt made to look like a tuxedo and a pair of black pants.

"I love your shirt," Lauren said. She couldn't look at it

without smiling. It was a nice touch in a sea of tuxedos.

"I wish I would've thought of that," Gavin said.

"Stick around, and I will teach you, young grasshopper."

Gavin laughed, and Rae shook her head.

"Have you checked out the games yet?" Lauren asked, feeling like she needed to tell everyone about the awesomeness that awaited them.

Tommy looked longingly toward the game area. "We were heading there, but Rae insisted on coming to say hi first."

"Excuse me for being polite," Rae said.

"I know such an inconvenience you are."

Rae gave him a dirty look, but it quickly warped into a loving affection.

"What table are you guys at?" Rae asked.

"Six," Lauren said.

"Us too!"

"Great. We'll catch up with you later."

"Let me take him to the games before he blows a gasket," Rae said, grabbing Tommy's arm and pulling him toward the games.

"They're adorable," Lauren said.

"Not as adorable as us," Gavin said, placing a kiss on her forehead.

"Please tell me this is the most amazing event you have ever been to," Lily May said in a rush. Her blonde hair was pulled back in loose twists and secured at the nape of her neck. The bright pink dress she wore was stunning and made her shine as she should.

"It's amazing," Lauren said.

"Really?" Lily May asked, lips parted as she let out a sigh.

"You need to calm down," Gavin said. "This is the best gala I've ever been to, and I've been to a lot."

"Stop it. You lie!"

"No," Gavin said with an air of sincerity in his tone. "It's amazing. You're going to have clients lining up to get you to work for them."

"Eep!" she squealed. "I hope so! Once this is over, I'll be back to being unemployed, and I won't be able to afford my rent."

'You live in the building your billionaire boyfriend owns. I think he'll let you slide on a few payments if it came to that."

Lily May gasped and slapped a hand over her heart. "Goodness gracious, I would never."

Gavin didn't push the matter, and Lauren knew it was because he understood.

"Oh no!" Lily May exclaimed. "They are not serving wine in those glasses. Over my dead body. Excuse me, I have business to attend to."

"Don't let us stop you," Gavin said.

Lily May hurried across the floor toward a waiter carrying a tray. After a brief conversation, the waiter and the glasses of wine disappeared before reappearing with new glasses that had an art deco feel to them and matched the event.

The attention to detail was insane but Lauren didn't expect anything less from Lily May. While Lauren was paying attention to Lily May's wine glass crisis, Gavin picked up a conversation with a couple whose outfits looked like they cost more than Lauren's entire wardrobe.

He excused himself and turned back to her. "Sorry about that."

"You don't have to apologize. I'm having a ball people watching."

"Always a guaranteed good time at these events. What we need though is alcohol. Where did that waiter go?"

"After Lily May sent him back to the bar to change the glasses, I saw him briefly, then he disappeared."

"I'm going to track him down. I'll be right back."

Gavin made his way through the crowd. He looked amazing in his tailored tuxedo, soft clean shave, and hair combed nicely into place.

Another waiter walked by with a tray of drinks, and Lauren grabbed two and thanked the man.

She took a sip of the cold liquid and closed her eyes, savoring the taste. This definitely wasn't the eight dollar bottle of wine she picked up at the local liquor store.

"You look lovely this evening," Ashton said, coming to a stop beside her.

"Thank you. You look pretty snazzy yourself." Lauren glanced around the event. "This is unreal."

"Lily May is the best and she really outdid herself."

"She did and I think this event will be the talk of the town for the next year."

"As long as it shines a light on the cause, then we accomplished what we set out to do."

Lauren really appreciated how Ashton gave his time and donated money to charities. It was obvious this particular event was really important to him.

Gavin came over and handed Lauren a drink. She gladly excepted it. "Did you tell her about what we worked out?" he asked Ashton.

"No."

Lauren tilted her head, curious as what they were talking about.

"Good! I spoke with Ashton earlier—"

"Gavin!" Pops stepped in between the group and wrapped his arm around his shoulder. "I want you to meet a friend of mine." Pops looked back to Lauren. "I'll only steal him for a minute. I'm sure my other son can entertain you until he's back."

Ashton nodded and Gavin and Pops walked away. Lauren took a sip of her wine and watched the sad clown trying to be cheered up by another clown.

"How's your foot?" Ashton asked.

She swallowed the big gulp of wine she took. "It's okay. Still hurts a little, but it's better every day."

"I know Gavin paid for your doctor's appointment, but we would like to pay any other medical bills you may have and we can pay you for your pain and suffering to avoid a lawsuit."

She stared at Ashton waiting for him to say gotcha, but he was as stoic as ever. Her eyebrows furrowed. "I'm sorry?"

"Would fifty thousand be enough? I'd need you to sign a contract stating you agree to the amount and to keep this quiet then I can get the check to you as soon as possible."

Lauren's head snapped to attention. "Excuse me?"

"I'll be frank. I don't want a lawsuit on my hands, so if fifty thousand isn't enough I'm sure we can come to a number that would make you very happy."

Lauren's head began to spin. All the times Gavin stopped by to check on her, to bring her things, she'd thought it was because he cared about her, but all he cared about was protecting his brother's money. Was this the deal he was so excited to tell her about? The wine she just drank felt like a pool of acid in her throat.

The night he closed the bar early, she was so touched. She thought he'd lose money by closing that night, but really, he was trying to save money by keeping her from suing him. Was any of it real? The kisses, the sparks, and the conversations. Everything that she had admitted to him…

She was an idiot. For a second there, she truly thought he cared about her. That whatever was between them was stronger than anything she'd ever known, but all along he was just attempting to keep her from suing him.

"I would like to handle this outside of the media," Ashton said, and all Lauren could do was glare at him. She didn't want his money and the fact that he thought so little of her made her angry and worse it made her sad. Money was the last thing she wanted.

Her stomach twisted, the hors d'oeuvres she'd eaten earlier now sitting like lead in her stomach. Tears pressed at the back of her eyes, and she waited for Gavin to pop up and denounce his brother's claims, but Gavin was nowhere to be seen.

Afterall this wasn't some story from her books. This was the cold hard reality. Gavin didn't have the same feelings for her that she did for him. All he cared about was his precious bar and keeping his brother's reputation intact.

Lauren met Ashton's green eyes and refused to be intimidated by the surly man. She imagined that he dominated the boardroom with his air of superiority, but this wasn't a boardroom, and she wasn't someone that he could break to his will. Not that he even had to. The only thing she was guilty of was falling head over heels in love with his brother.

"Thank you for the lovely evening. I hope you beat last year's record." She took off, hurrying through the crowd, and tried desperately to get outside before the disappointment and sadness poured over her lids. The last thing she wanted was to make a total fool of herself. Her shoulder made contact with someone, but she didn't stop. Didn't look back. Not even when she heard Lily May call after her.

twenty

Gavin finally got away from Pops and the person he'd wanted to introduce him to. He quickly headed back to where he had left Lauren ready to apologize for keeping her waiting for so long. Problem was, she wasn't there and either was Ashton. He looked around, trying to find the beautiful woman in that amazing gold dress, but amongst the sea of people, he couldn't find her.

He spotted Ashton with Lily May and made his way toward them. As he approached, he heard Lily May. "What was that about?"

Ashton shrugged, but he had that guilty look on his face.

Lily May's hands landed on her hips. "Ashton Oliver Mills, what did you do to Lauren?"

Gavin's heart slammed to a stop against his chest.

"I may have assumed something," Ashton said.

Gavin stepped in, grabbing his brothers' shoulder. "What did you assume?" Gavin said through clenched teeth.

"That she might sue you for the accident at the bar."

Gavin threw his hands out in front of him, anger and frustration crashing together in a fiery rage. "What is the matter with you?"

"Nothing, I was just covering my ass."

Of course he was because all he cared about was

himself and everyone else be damned.

Lily May shook her head. "Here you go again getting too big for your britches."

Gavin made it perfectly clear that Lauren wouldn't sue him because Gavin knew her. Lauren wasn't capable of something so petty. She didn't care about money or attention, the only thing she was guilty of caring about was him and now she thought he betrayed her.

Gavin tried to hold down his anger, but it was racing up on him faster than he could control it. "Did you ever think that not everyone is out to get you? That not everybody cares about your freaking money? Did you?" Gavin yelled, and quite a few heads turned in his direction, but he didn't care if he was making a damn scene. He was sick and tired of Ashton constantly thinking that every single person in the world was driven by greed. He needed to wake up and smell the damn coffee. "Lauren could give two shits about your money."

Ashton's regal façade wilted. "I messed up."

Gavin slapped a hand over his chest. "Did Ashton Mills just admit that he's not perfect?"

Ashton stepped toward him finger raised. "I have never claimed to be perfect."

"Haven't you?" For the last decade it'd always been about how great Ashton was, how accomplished and successful he was. Gavin couldn't escape it if he tried. It was everywhere, surrounding him and making him feel like he'd never amount to anything because, how could he? How could he be anything when Ashton was Mr. Perfect?

"No, I haven't," Ashton said. "If you think that, it's on you, not me. I have never claimed to be anything. I have worked my ass off to get to where I am, and I've made plenty of mistakes along the way. Shit happens. It's a part of life, and I'll be the first to admit when I mess up because I can man up and take responsibility."

"Oh!" Gavin exclaimed. "You're going to go there right now? You screw up, and you twist it back around to my mess up."

"Someone had to say it. If you would have manned up and got the construction taken care of, this never would have happened."

"You don't think I don't know that!" Gavin yelled. Anger melted into frustration and he thrust his hands through his hair. He should have gone to Ashton sooner. If he did this whole nightmare could have been avoided.

"What is going on over here?" Pops asked. "People are staring."

"Why don't we take this to somewhere more private," Dad suggested.

"Yes, please," Lily May said with a fake smile plastered on her face. She waved to a few people, that smile barely slipping from place. "Before people start to talk and the whole night is ruined. I love you both, but you are not taking this night away from me because you don't have the sense that God gave a goose."

"Huh?" Gavin said.

Ashton rolled his eyes. "She's calling us stupid."

"Do you have the handbook?" Gavin managed to crack

a smile despite the range of emotions battling it out inside him.

"What handbook?" Ashton exclaimed.

"Please go," Lily May said with another wave to the people. "And don't come back until you've straightened yourselves out."

Gavin had no intention of coming back unless Lauren was on his arm. He glanced at Ashton, still pissed at him. "I don't have time to deal with you. I have to find Lauren."

"Come on, I'll drive," Ashton said.

Gavin glared at him like he grew three heads right there on the spot. "Why in the hell would I want to go anywhere with you?"

Ashton ran his hand through his hair and let out a breath. "Because this is on me, and I need to help you fix it."

"You should have thought of that before you got yourself involved in a nonissue."

Ashton sighed. "I got it. Okay? Do you want me to help you or not?"

"You can't leave, this is your event."

"You definitely cannot!" Lily May said. "You can go in a back room and work out your issues, but you can't leave the premises."

"Babe, I have to," Ashton said. "I'll be back before the auction."

"You better be back quickly and things with Lauren better be fixed or you'll be sleeping on the couch tonight."

"Cross my heart." Ashton kissed Lily May, and Gavin took off with Ashton on his heels.

twenty-one

Lauren had never felt so unbelievably stupid in her entire life. If this is what she got for putting her books down and trying to experience life outside of the pages, then she never wanted to step away from the pages again. Heartache was bad enough when she read about it through her characters, but feeling it now, the empty pit in her stomach, the ache in her chest and the uncontrollable desire to find a corner and cry was too much for her to take.

She hated to feel weak, and right now that's exactly how she felt. Weak and pitiful because she fell in love with Gavin Mills while he kept her close so she wouldn't sue him.

Maybe she was overreacting, and she should turn around and go speak to Gavin herself. Ask him why he thought she'd want to make this kind of deal with his brother? Did he think that little of her?

Going back to speak to him would be the brave thing to do, the honorable thing, but Lauren was terrified of what would happen if it all turned out to be true. She'd be a pathetic puddle of emotion, and she didn't want Gavin to see her that way. She didn't want anyone to see her that way. There was a reason she bottled her emotions up. A reason she didn't open up to just anyone.

Tears pressed against her eyes, and she pulled her phone out and called a cab. She grabbed a napkin from her purse and blotted at the tears that managed to escape. She was mostly tear-free by the time the cab pulled up.

With a deep breath, she straightened her shoulders and climbed into the backseat. Her phone flashed with Gavin's name, but she ignored it. She had nothing left to say to him. All she wanted right now was to go home, get out of this ridiculous dress, and crawl into bed with one of her books.

She wanted to escape reality and pretend that tonight never happened.

As she paid the driver and slipped out of the taxi, she swiped at her eyes. Olivia and Ashlynn were probably sleeping, but if they weren't Lauren didn't want to have to answer any questions because she wouldn't be able to stop crying long enough to get words out.

She blotted her eyes one last time. She was halfway up the porch steps when she heard her name. Every muscle in her body froze. Gavin was the last person she wanted to see. She didn't think she could face him. She liked to believe she was a strong independent woman, but right now she felt weak and broken.

She continued up the stairs.

"Lauren, please." This time it wasn't Gavin, but she knew that voice too. If Gavin was the last person she wanted to see, Ashton was second on that list. He told her exactly what he thought about her a short while ago.

"I messed up," Ashton said. "Don't punish my brother for my stupidity."

She didn't turn around, but she stopped walking, listening to what he had to say.

"I've been screwed over time and time again, and because of that I always think the worst of people. I'm working on it, and I'm sorry. Please listen to what he has to say because I think you'll want to hear it."

She heard Ashton's shoes back away on the sidewalk, then the sound of a car door opening and closing. The car started and took off. Lauren turned around, ready to scream to wait, but though the car was gone, Gavin was still there.

"Hi," Gavin said. The usual ease of his features was pulled tight with tension. There was a desperation in his eyes that hit her right in the heart. She fought the urge to run into his arms. She wanted to believe Ashton, but for all she knew, they were doing damage control. Ashton was a calculated man and like he said he's been screwed over before. He knew how to prevent it, how to keep things hunky dory. This could be all part of his master plan.

"Lauren, I'm sorry about what Ashton said."

She shrugged, trying to hold on to what little resolve she had left. "It's okay. I'm just happy I know the truth."

"How can you even think that about me?"

She didn't have an answer. She finally opened herself up to someone, took the leap, and jumped in head first. It wasn't something she did, and the pain she felt in the last hour was more than she ever wanted to feel again. She felt her heart closing up again.

"Do you really think everything between us was because I was trying to keep you from suing me?"

"I don't know what to think." She wanted to believe it was all real because it felt real more so than anything she'd ever experienced in her life. She loved him, but he made a deal without consulting her.

He stepped toward her. "If spending time with you didn't mean anything to me, then why did I save this?" He reached into his pocket and pulled out his wallet. He opened the worn leather flap and pulled out the green construction paper that she made into a badge.

"You kept it?" she said.

"I told you I would, and I don't plan on ever throwing it out."

"It's just a piece of paper."

"It's not though. It was the moment that I realized I'd fallen in love with you."

She gasped, completely taken aback by his admission. He moved to her, taking her hands in his, the construction paper pressed between their hands.

"What about the deal?"

He looked at her a perplexed look on his face when he closed his eyes and exhaled. "You thought?" He opened his eyes and shook his head. "The deal I made with Ashton was that his company would sponsor the St. Patrick's Day event."

Realization was like a wave crashing into her, hard and fast. "It was all real then." She blinked up at him and he nodded.

"I love you," he said. "And I know how crazy that is because we haven't known each other for all that long, but they say you know when you know, and I believe that now. I looked into your eyes that night, and I felt this shift in the universe like things were finally lining up. I realized then that if I never talked to another woman again, I didn't care as long as I had you to talk to. I didn't care if you were the only person I ever kissed again because I knew the sparks that I feel every time our lips touch will never be duplicated. My entire life I've felt like I lived in my brother's shadow, but when you walked into my life, sitting at the end of my bar with your nose in a book, it was as if the skies parted and light finally shown down on me. When I'm with you, none of the bullshit matters. All that matters is you and me."

Her heart swelled, filling her with so much joy she could barely contain it. This man in front of her was everything she ever wanted and needed. "You talk too much," she said.

His lips pressed together, and his head tilted. "I don't know how to take that."

"It means I love you too. Now stop talking and kiss me already."

His arm wrapped around her, and he lowered his mouth to hers.

twenty-two

The bar looked exactly how Gavin had always imagined, and he couldn't be happier. The four-leaf clover banner he helped Lauren make hung in the corner above the ping pong table he always wanted. A chalkboard hung on the wall next to a dart board, and people gathered around both, playing, drinking, and laughing.

Leprechauns of all shapes and sizes moved through the bar with glasses in hands and smiles on their faces. Some were a little more glossy eyed than others, and Gavin hoped their good time wouldn't wind up making a mess of his bathrooms.

Devin sat at the bar in his usual spot, a new glint replaced the dead look. Gavin assumed it had to do with the fact he was currently in deep conversation with Olivia. Brody and his friends were cheering each other, and Gavin watched as Brody spilled his beer. He laughed it off, grateful for the beer spiller and his continued business even when the place looked like it was hit by an earthquake.

Lily May, dressed in a multi green colored skirt with shamrocks on both cheeks and green heels that were covered in glitter, stood with Ashton, who actually traded his monkey suit for a pair of jeans and a green t-shirt. Ashton was talking with Alex and Frankie, who had the slightest baby bump beneath her white and green t-shirt. Ginny,

Steven, Cassidy, and Jon were next to them talking to Rae and Tommy, who was in the middle of an elaborate story Gavin guessed by Tommy's animated arm gestures. And over by the table, unwrapping the multiple loaves of Irish soda bread for the contest was the woman he was absolutely head over heels in love with.

Her white sweater sat on the hem of her green skirt and had the word lucky written in green across her chest, and that summed it all up. Gavin was one lucky bastard. He didn't know what he did right in life to deserve her, but whatever it was he was grateful.

He no longer gave a crap about that stupid competition he created in his mind with Ashton. He had nothing to prove, at least not to his brother or dads. The only thing he needed to prove was his love to Lauren, and he planned on doing so.

He filled a few more glasses, then let Luca, his new bartender, hold down the fort for a bit as he stepped out from behind the stick.

Lauren's head bobbed to the Irish punk song playing overhead, and he came up behind her, wrapping his arms around her waist and pressing a kiss to her cheek just below the shamrock Lily May painted there.

"Hey, he said.

"Hey yourself."

"Do you need help?"

"It's time to start the taste testing. You can get everyone's attention."

"Why? We both know I won," he said.

She turned in his arms and cocked her head. "I wouldn't be so sure about that, buddy."

"We'll see." Gavin stood on a chair and whistled through his fingers. The entire bar ceased talking and turned in his direction.

"Happy St. Patrick's Day, everyone!"

A round of cheers greeted him, beer glasses flying up in the air. Brody's sloshed over his glass and gave Ashlynn a nice shower. Gavin laughed as she turned her evil eye on Brody.

"I want to thank everyone for coming, and I hope you're having a great time!"

More cheers exploded through the bar, filling him with pride. "We're about to start our Irish soda bread competition. Grab a piece of each, they're great to help absorb the alcohol, and then make a note of your favorite. Write your favorite down on a piece of paper and drop it in the treasure box," he said, pointing to the box Lauren had set up on the table. "Cheers!"

"Cheers!" erupted around the bar, and people hurried over to the table, grabbing up plates like ravenous beasts. Lauren squeezed her way out of the crowd and landed in his arms with a laugh.

"It's dangerous in there," she said.

"Good thing you got out when you did."

"I know if I didn't, you would have saved me."

"You know it," he said, bending his head and capturing her lips.

"You two are cuter as all get out," Lily May said from

behind them.

Lauren smiled against his lips, and he reluctantly pulled away, tucking Lauren against his side. The entire gang joined Lily May, and Gavin couldn't imagine that it could get better than this. When he was an old man looking back on his life, he would remember this day. It seemed so insignificant in the grand scheme of things, but this moment had been everything Gavin had been working toward.

He finally had a good relationship with his brother again, he was surrounded by good friends who he knew were friends for life, his bar was finally complete, and Lauren was at his side. He was so full of happiness he thought he might burst, and he did when the door opened and his dads walked in.

Pops looked across the crowd and spotted them, leading him and Dad toward them.

"I hope you don't mind, but I invited them," Lauren said.

"No, not at all," Gavin said, then met Pops in a hug. "I'm so happy you guys came," he said as he let go of Pops and hugged Dad.

"The place looks great," Pops said.

Dad clapped his hands together. "And it's packed!" he exclaimed, pride filling his tone.

"You're just in time." Lauren greeted each of his dads with a kiss to the cheek. "We'll be picking a winner of the Irish soda bread in about fifteen minutes. There's still some pieces left if you want to get in on the action."

"Definitely," Pops said then greeted Lily May and

Ashton.

"We both know that I'm going to win," Gavin said. He had got the recipe from Pops and had made five loaves, tasting each one until he got it absolutely perfect. He wasn't going down without the victory.

"We'll be the judges of that," Pops said. He and Dad disappeared into the crowd, and Gavin turned to Lauren.

He kissed her fast and hard, getting a whoop whoop from Tommy. He pulled back, and Lauren laughed.

"What was that about?" she asked.

"To say thank you."

"I figured you'd want them here."

He nodded. "It's more than that though. If it wasn't for you, this wouldn't have been possible."

Lily May cleared her throat behind him. With a laugh he turned to the feisty blonde. "You too, Lily May. I owe you." Lily May took her event planning skills to a whole new level, and the buzz she created alone was something he could never repay her for.

"Yes, you do."

Lily May was only one piece of the pie though. Ashton, sponsoring the event, gave Lily May more to work with.

His attention turned to Lauren. "But Lauren's the one who believed in this place, in me, when no one else did. She's the one that kickstarted this entire event."

"Extravaganza," Lauren said with a wink.

"Whoever helped, this is all you, brother," Ashton said. "You saw this shithole for what it could be and now the Hole in the Wall is going to be an icon in this part of town.

186

I'm proud of you," Ashton said, and though Gavin never thought he needed to hear his twin say those words to him, now that Ashton had, he realized how badly he did.

"Thank you," Gavin said.

"Now don't mess it up," Ashton said, and Lily May shot him an elbow to his side.

"I'm excited for trivia night," Rae said.

"Menace II Sobriety is going to kick ass!" Tommy said, referring to his, Rae, Alex, Frankie, Jon and Cassidy's team.

"Not if Tequila Mockingbird has anything to say about it." Lauren high-fived her teammates, Ginny, Steven, Ashton, Lily May and she kissed Gavin.

"It's on like Donkey Kong!" Tommy said.

They all laughed, then Gavin stood on a chair again and whistled. "You ate, you judged, and now it's time to declare the winner of best Irish soda bread, though we all know I won."

"Not so fast," Lauren called up at him.

She opened the treasure chest and started putting the pieces of paper into five piles. When she was finished, she looked up at him and smiled.

"Do we have a winner?" he asked and she nodded. "The winner is?"

"Brody!" Lauren announced, and Gavin almost fell off the chair.

Brody threw his arms in the air. "Hell yeah!' he yelled, high-fiving his friends and scooping Ashlynn up in a hug. Gavin waited for Ashlynn to deck him, but she laughed.

"Congratulations, Brody, you win a free pint a day for a

year!"

"Woohoo!"

The crowd erupted into cheers that quickly turned into an Irish drinking song. The entire bar sang, and Gavin joined his dad, his friends, and Lauren to sing along.

He wrapped his arm around Lauren and kissed her. "Are you having fun?" he asked.

"A blast. Except I really want to know what happens next in the book."

He let out a laugh that echoed above the crowd. He loved everything about today, but he couldn't wait for tonight when he was in bed with Lauren, reading to her from *The Two Towers*.

"You'll find out soon enough," he said.

"If someone can keep his hands to himself." She flashed a sexy smile at him, and he nearly melted there on the spot.

"Keep looking at me like that, and all bets are off."

"Only after you finish the chapter."

"Deal." He sealed it with a kiss. He pulled back and looked at her sweater, the word practically smiling up at him. Yup, he was one lucky bastard.

Like the book?

Leave a review!

Reviews are a great way to say thank you to the author.

More Sandra Coming Soon!

Fairytale Mash-up Series

What if the Seven Dwarves were the Princes?

Snow
AND THE SEVEN
Roommates
A FAIRYTALE MASH-UP SERIES, VOLUME 1
SANDRA MARIE

also by Sandra

Romance for all Seasons
After the Night
Across the Street
Under the Tree
Going Down
Between Friends
Behind the Stick

Summer Nights
Bay Breeze
Tequila Sunrise

A Fairytale Mash-up Series
Snow and the Seven Roommates
The Princess and the Doc
Tangled up in Zia
The Search for Ella
The Blind Date Beauty
The Rookie's Rebellious Hottie
Beauty and the Grump

about Sandra

Sandra Marie is in love with all things holidays and all things romance! After settling in with a big cup of hot cocoa—with lots of whipped cream—she spends her time with quirky and fun characters.

Romance for all Seasons is her debut series

Connect with Sandra

Become a Sandra Sweetheart
(Get ARCs!)
Join Sandra's Newsletter
Follow Sandra on Bookbub
Follow Sandra on Facebook

Made in the USA
Monee, IL
03 April 2021

63684750R00114